Alice

in Creepsville

Alice
in Creepsville

NORA ATAYDE

ISBN: 978-1-4269-3847-4 (sc)
ISBN: 978-1-4269-6414-5 (e)

Trafford rev.04/21/2011

 www.trafford.com

North America & International
toll-free: 1 888 232 4444 (USA & Canada)
phone: 250 383 6864 ♦ fax: 812 355 4082

1.

Welcome to A Brainwashed Town- A.K.A Creepsville

Creepsville is a small town, a town where you know everyone and everyone knows you.

A small town where you can leave your door's unlocked.

"Augh… what time is it?"

This is where I live, but I'm different from everyone else… well, my friends are different as well.

"Still too early…"

Here in this town, rich kid's wear whatever mommy and daddy tell them to.

I, on the other hand, have no parent's.

My parent's left me to do work over sea's when I was ten.

Now I'm fifteen and I dress however I want. The families here in Creepsville dress in white and navy blue, or any colorful color's, while I wear black, just like my friends.

I have only two friends, the only two kids I could save from, somehow, being brainwashed.

First, there's Anne. She moved here just four years ago.

Ever since I knew here she's loved wearing frilly princess outfit's.

One day, while on the computer, she found Lolita. Now she dresses like a Gothic Lolita.

Then there's Alex. He's lived here all his life, just like me.

He dresses in whatever, as long as it's black.

"I guess I should get up now."

I get up and trudge towards the bathroom, as if I were walking to prison.

"Cold water… on."

Performing my hygienic routine took only six or seven minutes, new time.

"Done… yay."

I quickly walk back to my black, Gothic princess room and try and find something to wear.

I'm awake now, so no sense in being slow now.

"Where the bloody hell is that shirt?"

After ripping through my closet I find the shirt I need and quickly change.

"Pant's! I forgot!"

Panicking in the morning is not good for you, it makes you forget your pants apparently.

Finally finding some black ripped jeans I quickly put them on, then finally putting on some old converse, a rose barrette and a bracelet.

"Okay, ready!"

I run back to the bathroom and check myself in the mirror.

A white, torn shirt with a large bat on the front, matching with my bat collar.

My pale face looked so small under my layered, jet, black hair.

"Perfect."

Just as I was finished the doorbell rang.

I ran back to my room, grabbed my book bag, run downstairs, almost slipping on the tiled kitchen floor, then finally running into the door before opening it.

"Oww...."

"Did you run into the door again? You know, you can be such a ditz in the morning."

"Shut up."

"Well good morning to you too Alice."

"Sorry Anne. I was in a bit of a rush."

"Well no worries, oh and look, look!"

Anne twirled around in a new black dress with red frill's and red roses around the hem.

She looked like a Gothic ballerina.

Anne is a beautiful girl, she was small and petite like me.

Her hair was jet black, and curly, perfect for her style of clothing.

Her pale skin and blood red lips made her look like a perfectly sculpted doll.

"You look really pretty Anne, like a Gothic princess."

"Why thank you."

Anne giggled and skipped away to her black VW, while I slammed the door shut and locked it.

Stupid door, it's old and need's to be replaced.

I quickly ran down the driveway to Anne's car, thankfully I didn't run into the car this time.

"Morning Alex."

"Oh, um h-hey."

Alex was wearing his typical band T-shirt with some Tripp pants.

Alex wasn't as pale as me or Anne, but he was still somewhat pale.

His eyes were a sky blue, or maybe crystal like… no matter how hard you tried to look away his eyes always drew you in.

I'm sure if he dressed like the other student's a lot of girl's would fall for him.

"The cloud's are always gray, it's not that I don't like it, it's just that it would be nice to see the sun every once in a while you know?"

Here in Creepsville the weather is always cloudy. It never rains or snow's and there's never any sleet either, but there's always clouds.

"So, since it's February…."

I could here Alex sigh, so I guess it was up to me to argue with her.

"What is it Anne?"

"Valentines day is next week, so I was wondering if we should go to the movies..."

"Are you serious?!"

Here we go, the daily argument between Alex and Anne.

"The movie theatres hardly have anything good horror movies on Valentine's day!"

As Anne and Alex argued over what to do on Valentines day, I decided to day dream.

Creepsville was covered with spider webs and bat's flied above-- WAIT!

"Those are real bats!"

Anne slammed her foot on the brakes and we all almost went flying forward.

"What?!"

I pointed towards the bats in the sky.

"Bats!"

We all stepped out of the car and marveled at the bats flying above.

Bats... this is totally weird, Creepsville is not a place for bats.

Why are they here?

"Awww, their gone now."

"I wonder what bats were doing here..."

"Who knows."

As we all entered the car, I couldn't shake a feeling I had. It was a feeling of... excitement.

"Ahh, the dreaded school. A prison for kids."

We all walked to our classes ignoring the usual glares at us.

Me and Anne said good bye to Alex and went into class.

Usually when we went into class a hush would fall upon the class but this time there was a lot of whispering.

"I heard it was a boy."

"I heard that too."

Such news… a new student.

The bell rings and the teacher comes in, I think he's smiling.

"Class, we have a new student. Please come in."

The class fell quiet as the door opened.

A pale boy with semi-long, back hair came in, but due to my short attention span I paid no attention to the new kid.

"Class, please say hello to Knight."

The class said hi then he said hi, yay we all get along…

"I hope we all get along."

2.

New Kid, New Victim

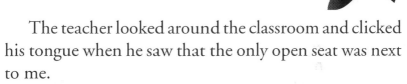

The teacher looked around the classroom and clicked his tongue when he saw that the only open seat was next to me.

"Well, for now sit in the back by Miss Parks."

I finally looked up when I heard my last name, and saw the new kid walking down the aisle to the desk next to me.

Looking at him I can finally see him clearly.

He's tall and quite pale, he has a some what baby face, but what drew me in was his chocolate eyes.

He was wearing a white collared shirt with either a blue or black under shirt.

His pants were a black dress type.

"Hello."

"Umm hi."

Ignore him, he's just another Creepsville drone.

"I can't believe SHE get's to sit next to him!"

Yeah, keep whispering you little--

"Class, please settle down, we have much work to do today."

The class settled down and the period went by quickly and with no problems.

The bell finally ran, and just when I thought I may go insane.

I try and get up, and when I do I have to wake up Anne from her nap.

"Anne… wake up!"

I kick her desk, which should be enough to jolt her awake, or at least make her think she just slept through an earthquake.

"Huh?"

"Wake up, class is over."

"Sorry, the classroom was so warm…"

"Is that so?"

"Did the bell ring?"

"I'm guessing… I'll wait for you outside."

"Okay."

I quickly walked out of the classroom and parked my pale butt by the wall.

I wish I could have napped, I don't think I'll make it to lunch…

"Ready!"

"'Bout time…"

As we ascended down the hall I could feel someone watching me. I turned to just see if anyone was tempted to do something behind our back's, no one was there.

I was going to look back and stop being paranoid but then I saw Knight. He was just standing there, staring at me, as if I were some kind of rare insect.

"Alice?"

"What?"

I turn to Anne, and pretend to seem as if I were listening.

"Did you hear me?"

"About what?"

"Augh! What I was saying was what if we just sat at your house watching some good horror movies, wouldn't that sound fun?"

"Yeah…"

I kept trying to look back at Knight to tell him off with some kind of imaginary power's, but by the time I was able to fully look back he was already gone.

The lunch bell finally rang, and we all met up just outside of the abandoned A-hall.

Due to some electrical and rat problems they abandoned the hall.

A-hall is just basically a long hallway outside with classes across from each other, with locker's between the door's.

You can actually see some decaying school supplies inside of them.

A-hall is the only place where we can get peace here, so ever lunch we climb the fences blocking kids off and set up lunch.

The rats had left a while ago so it's safe to eat there.

"What did you bring to eat today Alice?"

"Huh? Oh, I brought   water and a small snack really."

"Alice!"

"What?"

"You can't keep eating like this! Your going to get sick!"

"I'm fine, plus, I'm too laze to get up really early in the morning to make myself something decent…"

"Alice, I swear to Goth I'm going to--"

"Now, now girl's. It's lunch, let's relax."

"But Alex! She--"

"Fine, I'll go buy some pizza or something!"

"Thank you, at least that's something."

Before Anne can rant on about my eating I left. I think my ears were about to bleed from Anne's whining.

I swear, if she wasn't so loud she could actually be normal… in my book.

"Now… where do they have the red carts again?"

Spotting a red cart I quickly make my move. I'm not going to spend my lunch being taunted by these pathetic Creepsville teens.

"Can I have a small bag of Cheetos?"

"Coming right up sweetie."

I paid the cart lady and left. Even though it was cloudy here, it got hot pretty fast.

I wonder everyday how that happens…

"Hello Miss Alice."

"Huh?"

The sound of the voice nearly made me jump and drop kick his butt.

"Oh, hi Knight."

"You don't seem all that thrilled to see me."

"Because I'm not."

"That's quite cold, are you like this to your friends?"

"No, but your not my friend."

"That's true."

What is this guy playing at? I know he's the same as them, so why bother being nice to him? He'll probably turn around and stab me right in the back.

"What do you want Knight?"

"Nothing, I just want to ask you some questions."

I turn to face the annoying new kid, but when I saw his face it read 'serious business'.

"Can we talk in private?"

"What's wrong with talking in the hallway? Are you afraid I'm going to ruin your reputation by being seen with me?"

Knight looked, surprisingly, shocked. Like this was the first time he was ever accused of being of ashamed of something.

"Why would I be ashamed of being seen with you? I just need to talk to you, but it's private stuff."

Well the A-hall is pretty deserted, and plus if he tries anything I could just scream for Alex and Anne...

"Fine, in front of A-hall."

"Fine by me."

I lead the way, and I was trying to keep some distance between us, but it seems like he actually doesn't care to be seen with me.

Either this guy's bold or he's just stupid.

"Here is fine."

Knight looked around, and his face was back to serious business.

"Tell me something, have you always worn black?"

"Yeah. Why?"

"Just a simple question. Now, has everyone here always worn white?"

"Mostly, it is the main color, but it's not the only color."

"What about your friends?"

"What about them?"

This is starting to get way too suspicious. Not only is he bold enough to be seen with me but he's also asking about the dress code.

"Have they always worn black as well?"

"Yes, Alex was forced to wear white till I helped him out in buying clothes that he wanted. He just chose black."

"And what about umm…"

"Anne."

"Yeah, what about her?"

"She moved here like four years ago. She liked black already, she just loves wearing frilly things."

"Really?"

"Yeah."

Why does he want to know about Anne and Alex?

"And what about you?"

"Me?"

"Did someone inspire you to wear black?"

"No, I don't need anybody telling me what to wear. My parent's don't really care about me, so why should I care about what they want?"

"Do you hate your parent's that much?"

This guy was asking so many question's, and I don't think he needed to know the last one.

I was going to tell him to go jump off a cliff, but his eyes kept mesmerizing me. Every time I looked at Knight, I got the feeling of a wounded creature. Something that was afraid to reach out for help... afraid it'll get hurt.

"I don't... they just left me actually. When I was ten, they suddenly wanted to work over sea's. I just decided to stay here for Alex's sake. When he was a kid he needed help, he needed someone to back him up, you know?"

"Yeah..."

For some reason, it felt as if a huge weight was lifted off my chest.

I guess what they say is true, don't hold it in.

"I should get going back..."

"Okay, thanks for answering some stuff. I just wanted to learn a bit more about this place."

"Well... I'm glad I could help."

As I began to leave through the door's and into A-hall, I stopped.

I looked back at Knight... I felt kind of bad. I was mean to him, and he's a new kid.

He may not be so bad after all.

"Hey, Knight."

"Yes?"

"Why don't you come hang with us? Just for today?"

On that pale face of his, I swear I saw a small smile. "Gladly."

We entered through the door's and climbed the fence.

"Why is there a fence?"

"This is A-hall. The legendary abandoned hall. It's a miracle kids didn't break in to A-hall and spray paint it."

"Really?"

"Yup, it's the only place where you can get peace and quiet... if you don't mind the creepy feel of it."

"It look's wonderful."

"Hey, Alice!"

Anne came running up to me and grabbed my arm. Sometimes... she could be such a child sometimes.

"Alex said the--"Anne spaced off or she was staring at something. I turned to her point of vision and noticed that she was staring at Knight.

"You know that new kid huh?"

"Umm yes, it's a pleasure to meet you Miss Robertson."

"Oh, you already know my name?"

"Well we have first period together."

"Do we?"

"Don't mind her, she fall's asleep in that class a lot."

"Alice!"

"Well come on, I need to introduce you to Alex."

When I turned to walk towards Alex I saw him.

"Hey."

"How do you do that? I didn't hear you behind me..."

"He's totally being Ninja Alice!" Anne exclaimed.

"Alex, meet Knight. Knight meet Alex."

Knight held his hand out to Alex, but Alex just ignored it.

"Don't mind Alex, he doesn't trust people that easily. It's not easy to trust when everyone looks down on you."

"I see."

Knight smiled and took back his hand.

"I hope we get along Mr. Harold."

"Humph."

Well they seem to be getting along…

"Well how about we finish lunch?"

"Oh yeah!"

Usually when Anne remembers something, it's not good.

"Did you buy something good? I want you to eat healthy!"

"I bought some chips… is that good enough?"

"No, no, no, no, no, no, no, no!"

"Not good enough?"

Thankfully, Knight came in.

"What seems to be the problem?"

"Alice isn't eating right! Everyday all she brings for lunch is just water and a snack bar or something!"

"Well I eat something healthy for dinner."

"Oh yeah!? Like what?"

"Pasta, with some patties or sometimes a steak."

"But eating this much isn't really all that healthy!"

"Now, now Miss. Robertson, how about tomorrow I make sure she eats properly?"

"Really?"

Like that's going to happen…

"Yes. I'll bring her lunch."

"Yay!"

Anne ran off to eat the rest of her lunch, while Alex sulked and ate his lunch with her.

"You know, if you want her to really like you it's not that hard, and if you want to ask her out just ask her directly. She's not smart enough to get the idea."

Knight just chuckled and looked up at the sky, as if he were trying to find answer's to impossible questions.

"No, I want a girl who won't be afraid of my bite."

"What, is your bite worse than your bark?"

"You can say that…"

"Scary."

Knight chuckled and let out a yawn, and at that moment I saw something… interesting.

It looks like fangs, but I must be imagining it.

"You should eat a bit more Miss Alice."

"Huh?"

"Eating something small like water and a granola bar won't keep your mind awake to danger's. Plus… your blood will get bad."

"Is that so?"

I drank my water then looked up at the clouds like Knight did. I wonder if I could find answer's in this cloudy sky…

"How about we make a deal?"

"I'm listening…"

"If you eat healthy till the end of school year I will be your butler for as long as I live…"

"And if I lose?"

"Then I'll take you somewhere."

"Somewhere?"

"Where ever you want."

I thought about it. I mean, what harm can it do?

"Your on."

I finished the last of my granola and the bell rang.

"Lunch is over."

"Aww, but I wanted to finish my yogurt…"

"Just finish it after school Anne."

"No! It'll get gross by then."

"Just do whatever, hurry because we need to get to class."

Anne quickly ate as fast as she could and as we approached the fence, she ate faster than any hot dog eating contestant ever could.

"Done!"

Once we all climbed the fence we ran to our classes, and said our good bye's.

School had finally ended, and for some reason I felt energetic.

"Alice! Hurry the car's already started!"

"You guys go ahead, I'm going to walk today."

"You sure?"

"Yup."

Anne shrugged and skipped off to the parking lot. I went into the opposite direction, the less kids the better.

It felt nice walking instead of riding in the car. The air outside is natural.

My favorite part about walking home is that you could still be out by the time darkness settles.

"I guess I'll take a shortcut today because I totally forgot about Augustine."

Augustine was a cat my mother owned, but ever since my parent's left I've been in charge of her.

"I'm sure she won't mind if dinner is a bit late."

Half way home it began to get dark, for some reason I kept feeling an uneasy feeling.

"Alice parks?"

"What?"

Before I could turn around, a cloth covered my mouth.

"Got you…"

What the hell?!

"Where are you friends?"

It's kind of hard to answer you when your covering my mouth dude!

"You'll have to do for now."

The man pressed the cloth into my nose, and everything became blurry. The next thing I knew the man was being attacked by bats, and I could hear Knight's voice while I was on the ground..

I tried to speak and open my eyes, but my brain was not responding well.

"Alice… it'll be okay. Don't worry alright?"

I tried again and again to answer him, but no words came out.

Finally… everything went from blurry to pitch black…

3.

What A knightmare

I opened my eyes and was surprised to see that I was in my room.

I could have sworn I was walking home… when.

"Augh, no sense in fussing over it."

I get up and walk to the bathroom across the hallway, with a nagging headache following me, and begin my hygienic routine.

I washed my face and dried it, when I looked up in the mirror I… was somewhat speechless.

"My hair!"

My hair was bleached blonde, my skin was tan, and my nails were pink! Not a hot pink or a dark pink, but bright cheery pink!

"What happened?!"

All around me everything turned black then I heard evil laughter.

"Who's there? If this is your idea of a joke your going to pay!"

The man just kept laughing and laughing and I couldn't see him.

He stopped laughing then, I think, he snapped his fingers.

Suddenly, my hair was in a pony tail, I was wearing a white collard shirt, pink skirt and pink pearls.

"What do you think your doing?"

The man began laughing again, as if all this was a funny joke.

"Get these off of me right NOW!"

All the laughing stopped, and I was suddenly alone in nothing but black, darkness.

"Hello?"

As soon as I took my first step a black hole appeared underneath me. I began to feel like Alice in Wonderland, falling… feeling so confused…

I awoke in a different bed. A small bed meant for one person or two small people.

The room was different, definitely not mine.

"Where am I?"

The room was bare and had nothing but a bed, a guitar in the corner, and a couple of CD's on the floor.

By the bed there was a large window. I looked out the window and saw nothing but red roses, the backyard perhaps.

"Where am I?"

I looked around the room to finally see a pair of clothes with a note.

The note said the clothes were for me. I guess I should change, considering that my clothes are dirty.

I quickly changed into the new pair of clothes, which was a large white collard shirt and a large pair of sweats.

I opened the door slowly and quietly crept down the hallway. Once I reached the staircase I heard some muffled words.

I quietly climbed down the stairs and stopped when the voices became clear.

"Lucky we got to her on time, or else HE would have gotten her."

"That is true, but her friends weren't at school today."

"That's tragic news."

Knight is talking but... I can't figure out the other voice. It's a girl, I know that.

"So how is the young miss doing?"

"She's still sleeping. I hope she sleep's a bit longer."

"We need to find out the location of her friends."

Are they talking about Anne and Alex?

"In any case, we need to keep Miss Alice here till we find out exactly where her friends are."

What are these two talking about? It's making me nervous...

There's no way I'm staying here, while Alex and Anne might be in danger.

I went back upstairs and grabbed my clothes and my shoes. I quietly went back downstairs and tried to find a back door.

"This place is big enough to have a basement right? I mean, the room I was just in was the attic, so they had to have a basement."

I walked down hallways till I found a door that could lead to the basement.

I open the door and find another flight of stairs.

"Bingo."

I climbed down the stairs and turned on the light's. I was startled by the white sheets that were covering some square and oval items.

"I could have sworn you were ghosts."

I saw a window and found my way out, but my curiosity got the better of me.

I mean, who wouldn't want to know what's under those sheets?

"Let's see what's under sheet number one."

I lifted the sheet, and I was expecting to see some special box that may hold some remains of a mummy, but instead, I saw myself... a mirror.

"What the...?"

I uncovered the rest of the items and they were all mirrors.

"Why would he have no mirrors in the house and only in the basement?"

Whatever, I have no time for this...

I stacked boxes on each other and climbed out and made my escape.

I was finally on my street, and I moved quickly. I don't want to be attacked again like last time.

"Home sweet home."

I dropped my clothes on the couch and I immediately heard jingling and meowing.

"Hey Augustine, I'm sorry I didn't feed you."

I immediately went to the kitchen and fed Augustine.

I grabbed the house phone and check how many missed calls I had. I had just one.

It was from Creepsville High, what could they possibly want?

I was about to throw the phone till I saw the date.

"Hole bat! It's the fifth!"

I missed a whole day of school… how long was I gone?

"I should probably call Anne or Alex to tell them why I was gone, or at least give them some kind of excuse."

I called Anne's number, but it just went straight to the answering machine. I panicked and called her again, same thing. Then I called Alex, same thing.

I started to feel sick, what if I heard right and Alex and Anne have disappeared?

"Maybe I should go and check up on them…"

I looked to Augustine for answers, but she just kept eating.

"Thanks for the help."

I looked at the chili pepper clock on the kitchen wall, it was already dark outside, plus way past curfew for them.

Maybe I'll wait till tomorrow, I mean if I don't see them at school tomorrow then I'll go check up on them at their houses.

"Yeah… that's a good plan."

I took a quick a shower then went to sleep.

The next morning I got up and got ready faster than usual. I guess I'm nervous about what Knight said yesterday and with what happened as well.

There's no way they'll be missing right? It's a small, safe town…

"Yeah… I'm sure they'll be at school today."

Who am I kidding? I'm just making excuses, let's face it, all of this is suspicious…

That just means I'm going to have to investigate.

"Let's just hope none of it is true."

The doorbell suddenly rang and I ran to the door. A feeling of relief rushed through my body, but when I opened the door, it was once again replaced with fear.

"What are you doing here Knight?"

"You didn't say good bye."

I was about to slam the door in his face, when he smiled a sad smile.

"I'm sorry, I was just worried about you."

"Why? I'm fine."

"I know, but yesterday when I saw that guy trying to kidnap you I just…"

Well… he was worried about me.

"Come on in."

Knight finally smiled a believable smile and came in.

"Where's Miss Robertson and Mr. Harold?"

"That's what I'm wondering. I tried calling them yesterday but it just went straight to voice mail."

"Is that so?"

I glanced at Knight, his face was grave. He seemed to have a bad habit of spacing off when he was thinking about something serious.

"Do you have any idea to where they have gone?"

So he thinks I know…

"Like I said I tried calling them yesterday but it went to voice mail. I have no clue to where they are."

Knight let out a sigh, and my angry side got the best of me.

"But I'll tell you want thing, if some nut job kid napped them, like that guy did the other day, there's going to be some serious bone breaking."

"Is that so?"

"Yes. No one touches my friends and gets away with it. If they have a problem with them, they have to get through me to get to my friends."

"You care about your friends deeply…"

"We're all the family we got left."

Knight let out a sigh and spaced out. I decided that I should get my stuff and start walking to school. It's almost six so I should get a move. I skip upstairs then back down.

"Your getting ready to leave?"

"Yeah."

"Won't you be a bit cold wearing that?"

I looked down at my outfit. A red plaided Lolita dress with fishnets underneath. A gift from Anne.

"I'm fine. I just want to get to school on time and see if my friends are there."

I tightened my book bag when I suddenly felt something warm on my back.

I looked at Knight who was looking awkwardly and turning red.

"Just wear that for today."

Knight was wearing just a plain black ripped shirt with black jeans.

Not the kind of clothes he was wearing the first day he arrived.

I was about to give him back his jacket, but for some reason I held on to it, like it was my support.

"Thanks."

Knight walked me out and he closed my door. Then he lead my to a black car.

He first went to my side and opened the door and gestured for me to get in. So gentlemanly like.

"I hope you don't mind driving with me."

"Not at all."

Knight started the car and we were off to the teenage prison they called Creepseville High.

Halfway to the school I just remembered the way Knight was dressed.

"Hey Knight."

"Yes?"

"Why are you wearing all black today? I thought you dressed like the rest of Creepsville."

"No, this is how I normally dress."

"Oh."

I could feel myself turning red and suddenly feeling all nervous. This was the first time I've ever felt this nervous with someone, I hope it doesn't become a habit.

When we finally parked into the parking lot I saw Anne's car. Now a true rush of relief swept through my body.

"Anne's here!"

I heard Knight let out a sigh, a sigh of relief.

"Come on, let's go find them!"

Knight and I began wondering the halls trying to find Anne and Alex.

No luck.

"They might be in the abandoned hall you guys always eat lunch in."

"That's right!"

I felt anxious, and yet happy… I can't wait to see Alex and Anne's smiling faces.

"Stay here Knight, I'll go check."

Knight nodded and stayed watch for any teachers or students while I climbed the fences over to A-hall.

I searched and searched. No luck. I went inside of every abandoned class, no luck.

"Their not here."

When I finally got back on the other side the bell rang.

Me and Anne have first period together, so maybe she was in class already.

"Anne might be in class."

"Well shall we see?"

I nodded and smiled and followed Knight, whom I felt so safe with all of a sudden.

Finally entering class I saw a girl in the back with curly black hair, but it wasn't Anne.

She wore a white collard shirt and a navy blue skirt to match her nails.

Her necklace wasn't the ones Anne usually wore. This girl's necklace was in the shape of ice cream with a 'Kawaii' face on it.

"Umm excuse me."

The girl looked up at me and smiled.

"Hello Alice."

"Umm hi, this seat belongs to Anne Robertson."

The girl tilted her head to the side, like a confused puppy then smiled like it was a joke.

"Oh you silly! You had me going there for a minute."

"I wasn't kidding…"

"There you go again, I am Anne. Anne Robertson, don't wear it out."

No way… this can't be Anne.

I turn to Knight for answers but his face looked grave again and shocked at the same time.

I think Knight was just as speechless as me.

I turn back to the bubble chewing, giggling cheerleader of a girl.

This can't be the Anne I know… it just can't.

"Class please settle down!"

I sat in my seat, but I kept trying to scoot away from this Creeps Ville drone.

This wasn't the Anne I knew.

4.

Could This Be A Dream Within A Dream?

During first period I wanted to scream. There was no way that could be Anne! She's not like that!

What happened to the frilly Lolita girl I know?

"Alice…"

I turned to Knight and gave me an encouraging smile.

I smiled back but I knew that there was no reason to smile. My friend has finally either lost it or got tired of us. Five minutes later the bell rang, and I felt to sick to get up.

"Do you need help Miss Alice?"

"I'm fine."

I slowly get up and wobble to the hallway…

If Anne was like this, I'm afraid to see how drastically Alex has changed.

"You don't look well Miss Alice, should I take you to the nurse?"

"I'm fine, just let my legs get used to the shock."

"Don't push yourself Miss Alice, remember your a girl."

"I said I'm fine."

Almost immediately Knight lifted me princess style and took me out to A-hall. He put me on his back and climbed the fence.

"Knight! I said I'm fine!"

Knight put me down gently on a tree stump that was cut down.

"You don't look fine. Your more pale than usual."

"Don't be such a worr--"

"Did you not hear me? I said don't push yourself, your still a girl."

Knight put his forehead against mine the chuckled.

"That's good, you don't have a fever."

He stood up then looked around, as if people were watching us.

My head was spinning with so many questions, but there were no answer's.

Like how did Knight know that Anne and Alex disappeared? How did he know when to come and rescue me? Why was Anne...

"Miss Alice?"

I looked back up at Knight, which snapped me back to reality.

"I'm fine... I just wish this was a dream within a dream..."

I looked around A-hall, wishing that the old Anne would pop out of no where and say 'I got you!'.

"Why don't I take you home Miss Alice?"

"I'm fine, I'm sure I can last through out the whole day."

Knight gave me one of those 'Uh-huh, sure' looks, and again he lifted me up princess style.

"Shall I escort you home princess?"

"Put me down! I'm serious Knight!"

Knight ignored my screams and proceeded to the parking lot.

I didn't really struggle, it felt nice being held by him. It made me feel like a child again, and I noticed something I hadn't before… Knight had a faint manly scent.

"Okay, we're here."

Knight gently sat me in the car, as if I were a sleeping child.

"Thanks."

After he closed the door I buckled my self in and drifted off into sleep.

My eyes felt heavy, but yet I was able to open them. I was in my room this time. I thought this was that same nightmare again so I quickly got up and ran to the mirror.

Yup… same old pale girl with black hair and black finger nails.

I checked the time on my Nutty Batty clock, and it was barely passed one.

I should have a cup of coffee, that should wake me up.

I stomped downstairs and saw a familiar figure in black.

"Knight?"

Knight looked up at me in surprised.

"You up already?"

"Yeah… didn't really feel like napping."

"Is that so?"

"Yeah, I get the worst head aches when I wake up from a nap."

Speaking of which, I can feel it coming now.

"So what are you doing here? I thought you'd be back in school."

"I figured that you'd probably need me here, so I stayed."

"Thanks, that means a lot."

Knight smiled and got me a cup of water and some Tylenol.

As I was about to take the pill I could see something odd. Knight was standing in front of the small window above the sink… so where is his reflection? Could it be my head ache playing games with me? Or could it be the gray sky tricking me? Either way… I wanted an answer.

"Is something wrong Miss Alice?"

"Huh? Oh… no, nothing's wrong."

"That's good. Well I should get home."

Knight got his jacket and keys, said his good byes and left out the door. I quickly opened the door and grabbed a decorative mirror that was hanging and aimed it at Knight.

No reflection…

"No way…"

Knight turned to me and waved.

I waved back like an idiot then went back inside.

As soon as I closed the door, I sank to the floor. Could I really have seen it? Is Knight a vampire?

My mind suddenly flashed to the first day that Knight arrived here, on our way to school we saw bats. Could that have been because of Knight?

"No, no, no, no, no ,no! Your getting carried away again Alice!"

I banged my head against the door and got up.

It's probably tricks from the mind, you know, from losing Anne.

Yeah… that's probably it…

"Yeah… I'm just imagining it."

I walked into the kitchen and looked at the window, the one that Knight was in front of.

No sign of tampering. No, get a hold of yourself Alice! I stomped back into the living room and turned on the T.V. on high, that way the sound could drown out all my thoughts.

I let out a he sigh and relaxed.

"That's better… hmm?"

Something's off…

I look outside the window cautiously, nothing's outside.

"Must have imagined something again."

I turned around and see a tall guy in a black suit. The same guy that tried to kidnap me.

"I won't let you get away this time."

I try and run but he grabs me and throws me to the ground. While holding me down he looks for something, but luckily, he didn't have enough time to look for it because Augustine came to the rescue.

As the man screamed in pain from Augustine's scratches I quickly grabbed a vase, that my mother had randomly bought, and hit him on the head.

"Come here Augustine!"

I quickly grabbed Augustine and ran outside.

I ran and ran, but I had no idea where I was going. I came up on Aqua hill and realized where I had run to.

Knight's house.

"Best place I could think of."

I rang the doorbell and waited for someone to answer. Two minutes later, the maid that was talking to Knight answered.

"Oh dear!"

"Please… call Knight…"

She quickly let me in and sat me down on the couch and ran for help.

I guess in this house people are good at responding because Knight came running in not a moment to soon.

"Alice! Are you alright?!"

"I'm fine…"

I looked down at Augustine who was shaking, and bleeding.

"But please help Augustine first. She's bleeding!"

The maid came in quickly and took Augustine from me, and she left me with Knight.

"What happened Alice?"

"After you left I turned on the T.V. to relax, but something didn't feel right, so I looked out the window then all of a sudde--"

Before I could finish my explanation Knight swept me up in a hug. I didn't reject or anything, in fact, I welcome Knight's hug. I felt so safe with him, and it felt nice being hugged again.

"Every time I leave you alone something happens."

I looked up at knight and he looked like he hadn't slept for days.

"I'm sorry…"

"It's alright, just as long as your safe Alice."

Alice? No Miss? Was he that scared of something?

"I'm fine, but I didn't really have enough time to put some shoes on."

Both my and Knight looked down at my pale, bleeding feet.

"I'll go get you some bandages."

Knight left the room, leaving me alone to, again, have my head swelled up with questions but no answers.

I let out a sigh and cursed under my breath. Knight came in with bandages, gauze, and whatever you could think of.

"I'm fine, just a few scratches on my feet."

"I'm not taking any chances."

"Worry wart."

After Knight was done bandaging my foot he gave me another hug and looked me straight in the eye.

"Your lucky you got away, your still a girl, don't try and do everything by yourself… alright?"

I nodded and he carried me off upstairs.

"Is this your room?"

"Yeah, it's still empty because I just barely moved here."

So this empty room was his…

"Rest here."

This time I obeyed him, because he had such a serious tone it scared me.

"I'll go check on Augustine…"

Once Knight left the room I fell into a deep sleep that I hadn't had in a while.

5.

A New Day A New Plan

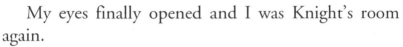

My eyes finally opened and I was Knight's room again.

"Oh… that's right."

I ran to Knight's house after that same creep broke into mine.

I got up and there was another pair of clothes for me, which reminds me, I need to give Knight's other pair of clothes back.

"What time is it anyway?"

I looked around, and noticed that the room looked more filled up. It looked way better than last time.

This time, there was a black dresser, a black book case that had a ton of books, and a computer desk.

"definitely looks better, but where's the clock?"

I quietly opened the door and quietly hopped down the stairs.

"Hello Miss Alice."

I nearly jumped to the moon and back.

"Umm good morning… umm."

"My name is Jenny."

"Oh, umm well, good morning Jenny."

This was the maid I saw Knight with yesterday. She looks too stunning to be a maid. With her looks she could be a model.

She was a bit tall, and her pale skin matched her, almost, silver hair.

Her eyes were a grayish green, and her lips were blood read.

She almost looked like a stunning woman you only see in paintings.

"Are you hungry?"

"Not really, I'm actually wondering what time it is."

"Oh, it's almost four."

"In the afternoon?!"

"Yes."

"How long have I slept?"

As I remembered about yesterday, a memory popped into my head.

"Where's Augustine?! She's fine right?"

"Yes, she's fine. She resting up in a warm bed in my room. Would you like to see her?"

I nodded my head furiously, I thought it might pop off.

She led me down a long hall that glowed red.

"How do the wall's glow like this?"

"The light bounces off the red wallpaper."

"Where are we exactly?"

"Well here, you may call it 'Luna Illuminava Hill', in English it would be called 'Moon Lit Hill'."

"This is Luna Illuminava Hill?"

"Yes."

Luna Illuminava Hill is Latin for Moon Lit Hill. It's a famous hill for it's glowing. They say on the night of a full moon, the entire hill light's up an Aquamarine blue, and it makes the whole place look like it's an underwater Gothic mansion.

Many people have tried to buy this land, but no one has ever succeeded.

"Here we are."

Jenny opened the door, and her room looked like a Gothic library, only with a bed in it.

The bedroom had two bookcases and a ton of magazines all over the place.

There was a wooden desk in front of a window, and by the desk there was Augustine. She was bandaged, on a warm cat bed, and sleeping soundly.

"She looks better than yesterday…"

"She kept trying to get up and run but I was able to calm her down."

I knelt down and gently pet Augustine.

Augustine has been part of my life so long that it would hurt if she just disappeared from my life.

"Well then, shall we let her rest now Miss Alice?"

"Yeah, she deserves it."

Jenny lead me back out the hallway and into the living room.

The room looked pretty classy. There were two couches of leather and a glass table in the middle. There was a wide screen T.V. and a couple of paintings. There's one of him and perhaps his parent's.

"Well Miss Alice. I must go, I need to go grocery shopping."

"Can I go?"

"Huh?"

Of course she's going to think I'm weird for asking, but right now, I don't feel like being alone in this house.

"Well, I have money with me actually, so I just wanted to go buy some clothes."

Jenny smiled and opened the door.

"After you Miss Alice."

"Please, call me Alice. The Miss makes me sound old."

"Of course."

Jenny led me into a nice purple car.

"Nice car, yours?"

"Yes, Mr. and Ms. Aoi bought it for me."

"Wow, their really kind huh?"

"Yes, they took me in when no one would."

"You're were an orphan?"

"You could say that."

Jenny started her car and went off.

Jenny finally stopped the car, and I realized that we were at the mall.

"Weren't we going to go buy groceries?"

"It's wise to buy materials first, then food."

"Very wise."

We got out of the car and headed towards the mall. Thank Goth that the extra clothes they lent me were pretty normal ones. A plain black shirt and black ripped jeans. Though, the jeans were a bit long, so my guess are that these are Jenny's.

Jenny on the other hand… was wearing a maid outfit. I don't really know how normal that is in public.

"So which store would you like to go first?"

"I heard that there was a new Gothic store downstairs."

Jenny smiled and we both walked downstairs. It was actually nice talking to Jenny.

In many ways she's just like Anne, just a bit more mature.

When we finally reached the store, we were in awe.

"My, I didn't know that there was store like this here."

"Me neither, I just heard it from my friend a while ago."

The store was small, but it was there. I think this was the best they could afford.

Not really the best town to open up this kind of store in, but, I'm still happy it's here.

"Come on Alice!"

Jenny grabbed my hand and dragged me in. Some of the worker's inside looked really bored, and they were dressed in all black, my kind of people.

"Hello!"

I never knew Jenny could be so full of energy so fast.

"Oh! Hello!"

Jenny quickly went to go look around while I went straight to the cashier.

"Umm hi, do you have any Gothic Lolita outfits--oh and some good T's?"

"Yes."

The man showed my a whole wall covered with frilly dresses and skirts then showed me some cool accessories. The, he then showed me some cool band T-shirt's.

"Thank you."

"No prob."

This is what I like about these stores. Not only are the people working here dressed cool, but they act as if they've known you for a while and treat you like a person.

"Let's see. What kind of ruffled dress would shock Anne out of her state?"

I looked and looked till I saw the perfect dress. It was black with pink ruffles, and it had hot pink skulls with bows just on the hem and on the sleeves.

"Perfect!"

I went to the accessories and got her a beautiful butterfly necklace, then I got Alex the sickest Slipknot shirt with a new wallet.

I looked to find Jenny, and found her in the corner, looking at some cute shirts with hoodies.

"What are you looking at?"

"I'm just looking at this beautiful necklace."

I looked at the necklace she was holding, it was a huge metallic heart with a skull and wings in the middle.

The necklace was truly stunning.

"Why don't you buy it?"

"What? I couldn't possibly…"

"Why not? You earned it."

"No, I couldn't. I don't have any money, and even if I did I'm trying to save it up."

I grabbed the necklace she was holding and walked up to the cashier.

"Miss Alice!"

"What did I say about calling me 'Miss'?"

"I'm sorry, but Alice--"

"No butt's, I'm going to buy you this as a friend."

"Alice."

Before Jenny could yank it out of my hand I put it in with the other stuff I was going to buy.

"Is this all?"

"Yes."

"That will be thirty two forty-five."

I gave the cashier my money and she bagged the stuff up.

"Thank you, and please come again."

"We will."

I dragged Jenny out of the mall and back into the parking lot.

"Here's your necklace."

"Alice… you know you really didn't have to."

"Well I bought it, you're my friend so I bought it for you."

"But--"

"No butt's, it's your now. Now, shall we get the shopping done?"

Jenny looked so speechless about the gift I bought her, I'm guessing she's happy?

"Thank you…"

"No prob."

We got into the car and drove off.

When we finally got back from shopping, it was already dark.

"Hello ladies."

"Master Knight! I would have thought you went out."

"No, I decided to wait till you guys came back. Need any help?"

"Umm, yes."

Knight grabbed some of the bags then helped me out.

"Thanks."

"So did you two have fun?"

"Yeah."

"I see that Jenny has a new necklace, did you buy it for her?"

"Yeah. She looked like she really wanted it so I bought it for her. I'm glad she likes it."

"What else did you buy?"

"I bought some clothes for Anne and Alex."

"For your friends?"

"Yup, I thought of a new plan. If I'm able to help them remember who they were, maybe I could help them…"

"Not a bad idea…"

"But I don't think I'll be able to get near them."

"Well let's wait till Monday. That's a better plan than going to their house, right?"

I nodded my head and grabbed some more bags.

That same feeling started to bubble inside me. Such nervousness…

"Need help?"

"No, I got these."

I quickly walked into the house and placed the bags on the counter.

This was the second time I felt that way, could it be because he was a guy?

No, Alex is a guy, and I can talk to him no problem… so why?

"Alice? I something wrong?"

"Huh? Oh, no, I'm fine."

"Are you sure?"

"Yes, umm… is that all the bags?"

"Yup."

"Okay, I guess I'm going to rest."

Jenny nodded and I went back upstairs and quietly closed the door.

Why am I feeling like this? I noticed everything about Knight, the way he smiles, or the way his face darkens when he's concerned.

I even noticed that his room was full of his scent…

"What's wrong with me?"

I sunk to the floor and wished over and over again that I had someone to talk to.

Anne and Alex were gone… and Jenny was always busy. There's no way I could bother her with my problems.

At these times… I wish I had my parent's to talk to…

"I guess I'm just going to have to figure it out on my own…"

I got up and wondered around the room. I should go home soon, I shouldn't make Knight sleep in a different room.

"I should check on Augustine first, see if she's healthy enough to travel."

I open the door and Knight is standing on the other side.

"Is something wrong?"

"No, nothing. I was just gong to check on Augustine."

"Really?"

"Yeah, and I was just getting my stuff ready."

"For what?"

"I was thinking of going home. I don't want to keep occupying YOUR room."

"Heh."

I was about to walk past Knight, but he slammed he hand into the door frame, blocking the door completely with his arm.

"What?"

"You are so hard headed sometimes you know that?"

"What?! This is your house! Why can't I go to my house?!"

Knight kept coming close to me and I back away to the point where I was almost cornered into the wall.

"How may times do I have to tell you this? That creep is a MAN and you're a Girl. You can't over power a man. Plus, if he knows where you live I can guarantee you that he'll probably try something again and you won't be able to get away from him."

"You don't know anything!"

I tried pushing Knight away, but I barely made him step back.

"I told you. You're a girl, you need to think about what you can actually do."

Knight came closer and finally cornered me into the wall.

"Yesterday, when you came running to my house saying you were attacked, I just about nearly lost it."

"Well I'm fine. I'm sorry if I made you worry."

Knight's face came close to mine.

"You know, your going to take years off my life."

"Oh? How so?"

I could hear my heat banging in my ear, it feels like it's going to explode.

"Your going to make me worry so much about you."

Before I could respond he leaned and pressed his pale lips against mine.

Suddenly, Knight cut our kiss short and left the room, while I was left to stand there... totally confused.

6.

Let The Game Begin!

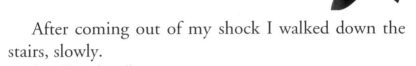

After coming out of my shock I walked down the stairs, slowly.

"Hello Alice."

"Hey..."

I looked around, trying to see if there was sign of Knight. I really didn't want so see him after what just happened.

"If your looking for Master Knight, he left just a while ago."

"Is that so?"

For some reason I feel... disappointed.

"Well dinner is ready, do you want to eat?"

"Yeah. I haven't eaten much."

Jenny led me into the dining room, which was a long table. The table was the size of three dining room tables put together.

"I made two separate courses. What would you like?"

"Umm, well, what do you have?"

"I have some steak and some really good Japanese food."

"What kind of Japanese food?"

"Curry and some other stuff."

"I'll try the curry then."

"Coming right up."

Jenny sat me at the table the got me some curry. After Jenny brought me some food she brought some drinks.

"Well pick here, and I guess that's it."

"Wait, your not going to eat with me?"

Jenny looked confused the just smiled.

"I'm not sure you would Like to eat with me."

"Why not?"

"I have… weird eating habits."

"Oh please, trust me I wouldn't mind."

Jenny smiled and awkward smile then went into the kitchen and brought out spaghetti.

She went back to the kitchen and brought a thick sauce for the spaghetti.

It looked so blood red I thought it was actual blood.

Maybe it was, Knight could be a vampire, I wonder if Jenny is one as well…

"Okay, but it'll be a quick bite alright. Plus, it is a little rude, since Master Knight isn't here."

"Umm… yeah!"

I could feel my face getting hot… I guess this is what you call blushing?

"Did something happen between you and Master Knight?"

"Huh? Nothing really…"

Jenny gave me a quizzing look, but gave up.

"So… where is Knight anyway?"

"He said he'll be going off to research something."

"This late? You'd think he'd be a vampire roaming around this late."

I looked up at Jenny, and she seemed to be paralyzed. Her face held such terror…

"What's wrong Jenny?"

"Nothing, I think I dropped some sauce on my uniform."

"Oh, you just suddenly looked horrified…"

"Sorry."

There were three vases on the long dining room table, and you could see the reflection of anything on them, but when you try to see Jenny's reflection, you could only see half.

Everything else showed up just fine, everything showed up whole… but Jenny showed only… half.

Maybe Jenny is a vampire or maybe human turning vampire?

"This curry stuff is actually pretty good."

"Thank you."

Me and Jenny began to talk about food and so on. I'll think about the vampire theory later. Right now, I'll just hang out with my new friend, jenny, and worry about Knight later as well. No need to rush and think about these kind of things right?

"Augh, I'm fool."

"Well that's fantastic."

Jenny suddenly looked up and put away all the dishes.

"What's up?"

"Master Knight is home."

Knight is home, and that my cue to leave.

I quickly walk to the end of the dining room and out the door.

Down the hall and almost reaching the stairs, I think I'm going to make it but my hopes are dashed.

"Alice…"

"Umm Hey Knight…"

Crap.

This isn't awkward at all…

"Did you and Jenny already eat dinner?"

"Umm yes. Jenny's a really good cook."

"That's good. Jenny tells me that you and her are becoming good friends."

"Really?"

Jenny said that?

"She hasn't had a real friend in years…"

"I didn't know that. Well I'm glad me and her are friends."

Knight patted my head and looked at Jenny, just coming out of the dining room

"I haven't seen her smile the way she does when she talks about you. I'm glad…"

Knight's face looked so gently when he was talking about Jenny. It's as if he loved her deeply…

"Do you love Jenny?"

Knight just kept looking at Jenny, for some reason my heart hurt and the same time I was pissed.

If he loved Jenny, then why kiss me? Is he just toying with me?

"You can say that, Jenny is special to me."

"Is that so?"

I was going to let him have, about how he loved Jenny but still kissed me, but Jenny was within ear shot and I didn't want to hurt her feelings.

"Fine, whatever. I'm off."

Before Knight could say anything else I stormed off upstairs.

I grabbed Anne's new Lolita outfit and stuffed it in a bag. I quietly crept out into the hallway and down the stairs. I checked the time and take off.

"If it's almost twelve I' going to take a while guess and say everyone is already asleep. Maybe there's a way I can lure Anne to my house…"

I walk down one street then another till I finally reach my house. When I was my front door trying to unlock the darn thing, I saw bat circling over my house. Then I had the sensation of someone following me.

I cursed a few words under my breath then turned it.

"Hi Alice."

"Anne?"

Anne was standing in front of me, dressed in all white. She looked like she was glowing under the quarter moon.

"What are you doing here?"

"Oh silly, you haven't been at school and I haven't been able to reach you. So I decided to pop by."

Anne kept giggling like a little girl and to be honest… it kind of scared.

"Why don't you come in?"

"Sure."

Anne kind of sounds like one of those 50's style teens. The ones with big puffy pink skirts with a poodle on them.

"So this is your house huh?"

"Yeah."

She doesn't even remember?

She has to remember something, because if she was a typical Creepsville teen she would just ignore my absence and not bother to come check up on me.

"What's that you got in the bag?"

I forgot about the bag.

"It's just a dress I bought today--wait!"

Something hit me in the head, hard. I smell an idea.

"Are you okay Alice?"

"I'm fine."

"So what were you saying? Something about a dress?"

"Oh yeah."

Perfect, Anne's right here, I can try to help her remember her old self with the dress. Perfect!

"Want to try it on?"

"Me? What kind of dress is it?"

I take out the pretty black and pink dress, and Anne's eyes are sparkling, but not her face.

"Here, try it on."

"I-I can't..."

"Yeah you can..."

Anne began to tremble and she kept muttering something.

"Anne?"

"White is the color, black is a big no!"

"Who said that to you? I remember you from before, you used to love black and anything frilly."

"No... no... I want to leave..."

Anne suddenly collapsed and landed hard on her knee's.

"I don't want forget..."

"Anne? What happened to you?!"

Anne suddenly looked up at me with wide frightened eyes... like a little rabbit.

"I'm afraid Alice... I can't seem to remember much lately..."

Anne kept sobbing and weeping, and I hugged her as tight as I could.

"My memory is so fuzzy, but I can remember parts. Like you smiling next to me, and another boy smiling beside me. I see myself staying up late making dresses that made me feel like a princess… but every time I do anything to help me remember… it hurts…"

Suddenly she stopped sobbing and she ripped herself away from me.

She stood up and looked down at me. Her face was stained with tears, her eyes were already red, and she was smiling.

"Oh dear, what happened?"

She's smiling as if nothing happened just now.

"Anne?"

"I'm sorry, I must have blacked out. How rude of me."

She was smiling like a creepy, horror movie doll and at the same time she was crying.

I quickly stood and picked up the dress.

"It's really late, maybe you should go home Anne."

"Oh, your right. Sorry for the intrusion."

Anne turned around and silently closed the door, leaving me alone in the dark.

I didn't know when I started crying, but cried. My chest hurt so much, to lose someone…. I already knew that pain. My mother and father suddenly became so distant, then they left.

Alex and Anne have never left me. No matter how many glares they get, or some good lectures from their parents they never left me. No someone want's to take them away… I feel like a child all over again.

I was too small to defend my self, and too weak to defend others…

"It hurts…"

I suddenly felt a presence behind me and I looked up at the mirror that was across from me on the wall, and saw the door open.

I thought Anne had closed it when she was leaving.

I turned to check if anyone was there and close the door, and again Knight was there.

"What are you doing here Knight?"

Knight let out a sigh and ran his pale hand through his long black hair.

"You…"

He's pissed…

"I thought I told you not to venture out on your own. You're a girl, and I'm sure that a man can over power you."

I began to cry, I couldn't stop…

I suddenly felt Knight's arms around me, hugging me tightly. All I could do is cry even more.

"Go ahead, cry it out."

After Knight had sat me down on the couch he brought a blanket from my room and covered me. I began to explain everything that happened and I could feel myself wanting to cry again.

"I see."

Knight just held me, and I felt safe.

I felt like a child all over. Every time I feel like a child it makes me remember such a bad memory…

"Why don't we go back to my house? I don't think it's really safe to be here."

I didn't answer him, so instead he lifted me and took me to his car.

He told the driver to go, and I looked out the window.

I can imagine a sad piano tune playing just about now...

Knight took me upstairs and left me to rest. I just felt too depressed to get up.

After the scene at my house I'm afraid. What if I pushed Anne further than what I did?

Obviously something happened... something or someone erased her memories and the same thing must have happened to Alex.

Alex... I wonder how he's doing?

"I guess I should thank Knight for bringing me home and comforting me, but I should give it to him for doing what he did."

I got up and wobbled towards the door. I quietly opened the door and saw Knight napping on the floor by the door.

I stepped over Knight and watched him sleep.

"Oh, Alice..."

"Hi Jenny."

I quietly stood up and walked over to Jenny.

"I just came to wake up Master Knight."

"Why is he sleeping there?"

"I suppose he was worried."

"About what?"

"About you."

"Me? Why?"

"I'm guessing... that he took interest in you."

"Interest? Wait, aren't you and Knight going out?"

"Hmm? No, me and him are just close, like brother and sister. He took me in when no one would."

'When no one'? What could that mean?

"Why don't you go and rest Jenny? I'll put Knight to bed."

"You can't! I mean-- you don't really know where he's sleeping."

"He can sleep in his room, I'll just sleep in the living room."

I turned around and walked away before Jenny could object.

I gently put Knight's arm over my shoulders and tried to lift him.

"Boy your heavy…"

Somehow I managed to put him in his original bed and I covered him and left him to sleep.

When I walked out of the room I noticed Jenny was no longer there, so I decided to go on to the living room.

It's almost two in the morning, I should get some rest.

"I'll just use a my jacket to blanket myself--"

I suddenly got a chill up my spine, I looked around and no one was there.

I looked around, nothing.

I finally was about to quite and go to sleep till I saw a tall dark figure outside the window.

He was just standing across the street… staring at me.

It was that same creep who attacked me twice.

He smiled, and I could see glistening fangs.

Could he be a vampire?

"Wait… on the day he attacked me, Alex and Anne disappeared also!"

I quickly ran to the front door, not before grabbing at least an umbrella.

"Come on out creep!"

By the time I was outside… he was gone.

"Coward."

I turned around to go back inside, but he when I did he was behind me.

Fear rushed through my body and I couldn't move. Good thing instinct took over.

"Get away from me!"

I hit him as hard as I could with the umbrella and it knocked some of the air out of him.

I tried to run past him but he got back up and yanked my hair.

I quickly fell to the floor feeling dizzy.

"Don't think you could get away from me this time."

He picked me up and I tried to kick, but he retaliated with a foot in my gut.

I felt nauseous and dizzy.

"Let… go…"

"You're a fighter, but I know what to do with humans like you."

Humans? What is he, a demon?

I kept trying to fight back, but he just kept walking on.

I tried on last time and I was finally able to get free. I ran and ran.

Just like last time I had no idea where I was going.

I ran till I finally bumped into someone.

"I'm sorry--"

"It's fine..."

"Alex!"

Alex... the one person I haven't seen in days-- and he's wearing black Tripp pants!

"Alice?"

"Alex!"

I couldn't contain my happiness and I tackled him.

"U-Umm Alice... don't you think this is a little awkward?"

I finally realized what I just did and quickly get off of him and help him up.

"I'm sorry, I'm just so happy to see!"

"Did the same thing happen to you?"

"Got attacked by some creep? Yeah, the same thing happened."

Alex suddenly hugged me then grabbed my face.

"Are you okay?! He didn't hurt you did he?!"

"I'm fine..."

I hugged Alex once more, I hugged him tight... as if he was going to disappear again the minute I let go.

"What are you doing here Alex?"

Before Alex could answer me I could hear loud thumping of footsteps.

"Where are you, you little brat?!"

"Crap."

I quickly grabbed Alex's hand and dragged him up hill, towards Knight's house.

When we finally arrive, I quickly get us inside and lock the door.

I turned on the light and sat Alex on the couch.

"Oh my..."

I was finally able to notice Alex's face, and it looked like he was beaten badly.

"What happened?! Are you okay?"

Alex tried to look away from me, but I wouldn't let him.

"First, you tell me where you got that bruise on your neck from."

I quickly go to the window for a reflection, and I did have a bruise.

"Like I said, I was attacked by some creep just now. I just got away from him. Second time may I add."

"Second?! When--"

"Hey, the deal was that I told you what happened then you tell me what happened to you."

Alex let out a sigh and tried to wipe off some dry blood from his mouth.

"Wait, let's wash you off first."

I dragged him into the kitchen and got the first aid kit.

"So what happened?"

I began to disinfect some of cuts and wash them out.

"It happened when you decided to walk home. Anne was talking about something then out of nowhere another car slammed into us. We were able to get out but then some thugs tried kidnapping us. We tried to fight but Anne was overpowered by one of them and they put me in some kind of cuffs."

"Then what happened?"

"Oww, then me and Anne got separated and placed into separate rooms. They turned on some speakers with a really high frequency. I thought my ears would bleed from listening to it. Oww…"

"Sorry, then what?"

"Then I guess they weren't doing what ever they were doing right. So they dragged me out of the room, I tried to resist and escape. I was able to escape and I ran. I finally saw a huge window and I saw Anne in a white room. She had her ears covered and she kept rocking back and forth. Again and again I banged on the window but she couldn't hear me. Then those same thugs caught me and they punched me hard on the face. I kept fighting back then they punched me hard in the gut. Oww that stings."

"Sorry, I'm just trying to help. Go on."

"I passed out, when I woke up a pale man kept talking to me, his words… it sounded worse than that high pitched crap. I felt sick, he finally realized I was trying to block him out. He suddenly slammed his palm against my face and kept whispering in my ears. I don't remember the words, but I'm guessing he was trying to make me forget, because my vision kept getting blurry and my memories started to flash before my eyes then disappear. Again I tried to resist. Thank god someone called him away and he left me alone. I ignored the puking sensation and I tried to knock the door down but it didn't work."

With every word Alex kept saying I kept wanting to hear more and at the same time I was terrified.

"So then I tried climbing through the air vents and that's how I got out. I just kept walking till I bumped into you."

"So what about Anne?"

"I don't know, I tried her house, but as usual the 'She's not home routine'."

"Actually… I saw her today."

"Really? Is she okay?!"

I explained everything to Alex about what happened, and he was as shocked as I was.

"What the hell were they trying to do to you?"

"I'm not sure but… Alice?"

"Yeah?"

To distract myself a bit I was trying to open a plaster aid when Alex said words that rang in my eras.

"The man that ordered those guys to abduct us was named Aoi, his last name I suppose. Sound familiar?"

Knight Aoi…

7.

What Is The Real Truth?

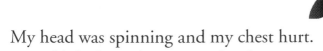

My head was spinning and my chest hurt.

I couldn't have been Knight, but ever since he came... all this did start to happen.

"Alice?"

I can't be crying again... why?

"Alice are you--"

The light's flickered on and Knight was standing on the opposite side with a really pissed off expression.

"Alice?"

Knight came over to us, and when he tried to hold me... I pushed him away.

"What did you do to her Knight?"

Alex and Knight began to argue, but I couldn't hear any of it. My head hurt, just like my chest. The tears wouldn't stop.

"Come one Alice. Let's go back to your house."

"Alice--"

Morning was coming, and the was the brightest part of the day. The sun was bright and shining. If Knight's a vampire, there's no way he would follow us.

And I was right.

Knight stopped just at the door and didn't even come after us.

When we finally reached my house Alex sat me down on the couch and went to go and get something for me.

I tried and tried... why wont these damn tears stop!?

"Are you okay Alice?"

No... I'm not okay!

"Let's go up to your room so you can go rest."

Alex helped me up to my room and before I got to bed I showed him the clothes I bought him and some extra ones as well. I told him where to take a shower and where the food is just in case he got hungry.

As soon as I was behind my door and into my bed the tears came again.

Why wouldn't they stop? Every time I closed my eyes, I saw Knight.

"Why does it hurt?"

I cried and cried till I finally fell asleep.

When I woke up, it was five in the afternoon.

I overslept once again.

I got up and went to the bathroom, and I looked terrible. My eyes were red and I head a really bad case of bed head.

I turned on the shower and got in.

It felt nice to take a shower in my own house.

"I guess I should check on Alex…"

After the shower I put on some black shorts and a gray shirt, I didn't even bother to dry my hair.

"Alex?"

I looked in all the rooms, but he was no where in sight. Fear crept in… what if that creep came again? What if he took Alex?

"No…"

I ran downstairs and saw Alex making something to cat.

"Hey, sorry. I was making us something to eat, I heard you in the shower so I got up and made us some-- are okay?"

Alex came close to me and lifted my face up.

"What happened? Did you have a bad nightmare?"

More like a Knightmare…

"I'm fine."

Alex made some pasta with Alfredo sauce or whatever and we ate happily.

It still felt empty… maybe because we're missing a chatty Lolita?

"How about we watch some T.V., that should get your mind off something's."

"Yeah."

I looked out the window and saw really cloudy clouds. It might rain today…

"What do you want watch?"

Alex sat down, and when I was about to sit down with him I felt a presence.

I looked around and saw no one, then the door flew open.

Suddenly, an angry Knight was appeared.

"You again? You bastard. As if you couldn't get enough out of brainwashing Anne, you have to come and torture us?!"

Knight stomped his foot in Alex's chest and had an aura of blood.

"What's your problem Knight?"

"You little-- your working for HIM huh?"

"Stop you two!"

I pushed Knight off of Alex and helped him up. Knight hurt me enough, he took my best friend from me... and I don't know how to bring her back without breaking her.

"How could you defend him Alice? He's not your friend anymore!"

"Shut up! You're the one that isn't my friend anymore! I hate you!"

I looked up at Knight, and he had the look of a pissed off guard dog and a wounded bird.

"Your part of this whole plot aren't you? You have some connections don't you? This is all part of some sick twisted plan of yours isn't it?"

"What are you talking about Alice?!"

"Shut up! Alex said he kept hearing the name Aoi! Isn't that YOUR last name?!"

Tears... why now? Why not cry after this?

"Alice you don't understand..."

"Shut up! Just leave us alone!"

For a minute, there was silence, the Knight kicked a vase.

"Fine, do whatever the hell you want."

And with that... he left.

I collapsed to the floor and cried, cried like the little cry baby I am. Is this really a brainwashed town? Have I been right all along?

"Are okay Alice? That guy is such a creep."

Knight... it suddenly hit me why I'm crying so much.

I know now why it hurts a lot... it's because... I love Knight.

8.

I Want To Stay Home...

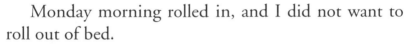

Monday morning rolled in, and I did not want to roll out of bed.

There's no reason why I should get out of bed... Anne is doesn't remember we're friends and Knight, my first love, will probably be there, and right now, I really don't feel like seeing his face.

"Wake up Alice, it's five thirty and we have to walk to school."

"Why are you up early? Your usually the last one we pick up because of you being so reluctant to get up in the morning."

"Well, that was back then and this is now."

"Is that so?"

After I kicked Alex out of my room I got dressed and did my hygienic routine.

Has Alex always been such a pest?

Back in my room I was putting my shoes on, and I saw Knight's jacket hanging on a chair.

I shouldn't think of Knight anymore.

"Are you done Alice?"

"Yeah… I'm done."

I grabbed my stuff and we were off.

When we arrived to school first period had already started, and Knight was not in sight.

Anne must have taken the day off or something.

"Isn't this a suckish day…"

For the rest of the day I walked to class like a zombie till Alex caught me during lunch.

Something was a bit off about Alex, but I can't pinpoint it…

"Ready for lunch?"

"Yeah sure?"

"What's up with you little miss gloomy bear?"

"What did you just call me?"

"Little miss gloomy bear?"

"Are okay?"

"Yeah, I'm fine."

Sure…

"So have you heard from Knight?"

"No…"

I said some really awful stuff to him… maybe I should--

"You shouldn't worry too much about that guy. If he's the cause of all the bad things that's happened to us."

"Yeah… your right!"

Why should I worry about that cold hearted vampire?!

The sad part of all this though is that one, Anne might not be my friend anymore, and two, I might have missed the opportunity of a life time hanging out with real vampire's-- if they are real vampires.

"Alice."

"What?"

"The bell rang, didn't you hear?"

"No, I'm sorry."

Alex began to clean up his trash while I cleaned up mine. Usually Anne would be rambling on about her next class…

"Hey Alice, check it out! It's a bat!"

I quickly looked up and saw a small cute bat perched on a tree. It looked at me with huge, brown, pleading eyes and I looked back at it.

When I looked at the bat… I could feel a familiar presence.

"Weird huh? This town rarely has bats."

"True huh?"

Alex went to clean up the rest of his trash while I stood there and looked at the bat.

"Aren't you the cutest thing?"

I was about to pet it, but all of a sudden it started squeaking and flew around.

"What's wrong?"

"The bat is just a bit scared…"

I turned towards Alex who was suddenly holding a metal bat.

He swung and I dodged,

"Alex?! What's wrong?!"

The bat kept circling over my head and I finally realized it.

Knight was protecting me.

"Stop Alex! What are you doing?!"

I started running towards an empty classroom but it was locked.

Usually they weren't locked, Alex must have done this.

"Stop running!"

I turned back to Alex, then he swung the bat. It hit my head and the next thing I feel is dizziness.

I didn't know a bat hitting against a humans head would sounds just like it hitting a baseball.

"Sleep easy Alice, you'll be peace at mind soon enough…"

"Alex…"

Before passing out I could hear myself swearing at Alex… and wishing I had stayed home… wishing I had stayed with Knight…

"Good night, my sweet Alice."

Alex turned to grab some hidden rope, so while he had his back turned I got up and ran.

I quickly climbed over the fences on the other side of the hall, the ones that led to the parking lot.

I could hear climbing the fence behind me, I tried to run but I could hear him getting closer.

"Damn it! Where's the best shortcut?"

Before I could decide where to go next I felt an arm grab me. I was about to scream till a small pale hand covered my hand.

"Quiet M-- Alice."

I nodded and Jenny let go of my mouth.

"What are you doing here Jenny?"

"Master Knight sent me."

"Knight did?"

"Yes. He was worried about you so he sent me."

I looked down at the ground and I felt ashamed of myself. For not believing in Knight.

"So shall we go?"

"Let's."

Jenny helped me up then helped me to her car.

"Are you okay so far Alice?"

"I'm good."

Jenny jumped into her car and we sped off.

Half way up the hill I just remembered something.

"Why didn't Knight come pick me up?"

"He was… busy."

"With what?"

"I don't really know."

"He's probably sleeping in his coffin…"

Right when we were in front of Knight's house Jenny slammed the brakes and gave me a horrified look.

"Miss Alice? Are you serious?"

I casually looked at Jenny, and she looked pale than usual.

"About what?"

"About what you just said."

"Yeah, why?"

"How long have you known?"

"It was just a theory, but you just proved it."

Jenny sat there quietly, till she let out a sigh.

"Please don't tell Master Knight."

"I wouldn't dream of it, but everything makes sense now."

"What do you mean?"

"Why he was tired half the time, why he didn't show up in reflections, and why he can walk around in Creepsville. It's always cloudy, it's a miracle if you ever see the sun."

"That obvious huh?"

"To me it was. I keep my eye open for this kind of stuff. I'm the kind of person who dreams of meeting a vampire."

"I can picture that."

Jenny put her car in the garage and I could tell she was still shaky.

"So what about you Jenny?"

"What about me?"

"Are you a vampire too?"

"You could say that..."

"You said before that Knight's family were the only people who would take you in."

"Yeah. They stood up for me in the vampire society."

I could tell that Jenny wasn't up to telling me.

"Just tell me when you feel like--"

"No! I want to tell you. We're friends aren't we?"

I nodded and stood next to her, afraid to move.

"So go on."

"Well the reason why people and vampire's didn't want me was because I'm a half breed."

"Half vampire half human huh?"

"It's not fair... why couldn't have I been born human? My mother was a beautiful model... I wanted to be just like her, but when I found out that I couldn't show up in some picture's..."

Jenny finally began to cry and I hugged her as tight as I could. It must feel awful being half of something and not being full, especially in her case.

"Let's go in alright?"

"Right..."

Once inside I made Jenny go back to her room while I went to go wash off the dried blood in my hair and face.

"Ick is all I can say. Geese that Alex, he left a bump."

I tried touching the bump but it hurt too much.

"Screw this this..."

I threw the rag back in it's place and went out into the backyard.

Even thought this place had no one living in it, the backyard still looked gorgeous.

There were beautiful roses and other flowers. The grass was green and there was two trees that made everything look a bit better.

The best place about this backyard was that it had no water fountain or bird bath, it was just normal plant life. Not something man made.

"This place looks like a nineteenth century castles backyard."

I looked around and noticed some bats hanging or sleeping on the tree branches.

It gave the place a spooky feel, the one thing missing is some dead plants.

I guess I'll--

"There's a table and chairs…"

I go over to where the white chairs and table are. I sat in one and looked around.

It really felt peaceful.

"Alice?"

I looked behind me to see Jenny, all better.

"Hey Jen."

"I see your enjoying the backyard."

"Yup, it looks peaceful."

"Master Knight loves to have tea here."

"Does he?"

"Yes."

"That's a surprise."

"You don't sound surprised."

"I guess I kind of already knew."

Jenny got up and left. A few moment's later she came back with tea and crumpets.

"You Know Alice, I think you might have some kind of sixth sense."

"Not really. I'm just sensitive to stuff."

"Heh, well I could see why Master Knight likes you."

Knight likes me?

"He worries about you a lot you know?"

"I worry about him too."

Jenny let out a little giggle.

"Well I think you two make the cutest couple."

My chest suddenly felt tight, but I felt really happy.

"Are you tired Alice?"

"Yeah, but I should probably do something about this bump first."

"Wait right here."

While I waited, I drank some tea and ate some crumpets. Jenny really is a good cook.

"Here we are."

Jenny brought some kind of ice pack and put it on my head.

"Here we go. That's much better."

"Thanks Jenny."

Jenny led me into the living room and laid me to res there.

"Sorry. I totally forgot about the rooms. I should really get to setting them up."

"It's fine. I just need a quick nap. You should get one too, you look like the dead."

"Don't you mean undead?"

I smiled and she giggled. She brought me a blanket and turned off the light's.

"Oh, Alice?"

"Yeah?"

"I'm glad your okay."

"Thanks."

And with that, she left.

Jenny had laid me down on the couch in front of the large window. The clouds looked like a menacing gray, something bad might happen...

"I should get some sleep. Alex wouldn't dare come here or that creep."

I closed my eyes and drifted off to sleep.

I could feel someone caress my bump, and when I opened my eyes I saw a pale boy.

"Knight..."

"Morning..."

I looked at the small clock perched on top of the fireplace.

It's nine.

"Crap, it's this late?"

"Sorry... I just wanted to let you sleep a bit more."

I could tell that Knight was still worried about me, he smiled and I sat up.

"I'm sorry..."

"About what?"

About what? Are you serious? I said some really awful things to you!

"About what I said yesterday. I didn't mean it and... thank you. Thank you for worrying about me and taking care of me these past few days."

Knight carefully hugged me and I hugged him tightly. I was afraid if I let go of him he would disappear.

"I'm just glad your safe."

Knight suddenly got up and went into another room then came back.

"What's that for?"

"It's for you."

"For me?"

"Yes."

Knight grabbed my hand and led me up to his room.

"Here, change into this."

"Okay…"

He then closed the door and I heard him walk away.

I took out some clothes that were in the bag and I was in complete awe.

It was a small white shirt with a black bat and a skirt to match.

It came along with stockings.

"This looks amazing!"

I then heard a nock at the door and opened it.

"Hello Alice."

"Jenny? What are--"

"Just come with moi."

"Umm okay…"

Jenny dragged me down the hall then into a bathroom.

"What are we--"

"Shall we get you ready for a bath?"

"WAIT JEN--"

Before I could finish my sentence Jenny had already started to rip off my clothes then she picked me up and put me in the bath tub.

"I could have done all this myself you know?"

"Oh but Alice I'm so excited right now."

"That doesn't mean you can use vampire muscle on me."

"Sorry. Anyways here are your fresh change of clothes a towel and I'll be back in ten to get your hair ready."

"Wait Jenn-"

By then the air head of a half vamp was out the door.

"I think in some ways she could be worse than Anne."

I looked around the bathroom and saw that it was porcelain white, just like mine, but the bath tub was different. It was one of those old style ones that weren't glued to the wall.

This bathroom is totally different from the other one I've been taking a bath in.

"I guess I'll just wash up then…"

I held my breath then went underwater. Then I resurfaced.

I grabbed the shampoo then the conditioner.

I washed my body then rinsed then got out. I quickly got dressed before Jenny could come back in and dress me herself.

"Now that's a scary thought."

I wonder how I look with this outfit on…

There weren't any mirrors in the bathroom's either.

"Knock knock! Are you done in there Alice?"

"Yeah."

Jenny quickly came in and started drying my hair. She sprayed some weird stuff on my hair, no matter how many times I told her not to.

"Relax. It's just to make the hair look a bit more shiny."

"That's nice…"

After Jenny was done using me as a dress up doll she led me downstairs and into the backyard, where Knight was waiting with a candle lit dinner.

"Knight…"

I heard Jenny giggle then walk away. I was too shocked to even move.

"Shall we sit my beautiful rose?"

"U-Um sure…"

I'm totally nervous right now! Can't my legs even function or is it my brain?

"Did you do all this for me?"

Knight chuckled and pulled the chair out for me.

"Of course."

Knight grabbed a white chair and placed it next to me.

He then sat down and smiled like a Gothic prince would. I could feel my stomach full up with butterflies.

"Sorry I just wanted to move closer for a better view."

Knight began talking and we had this whole normal conversation while eating steak and chocolate covered strawberries.

"The moon looks beautiful doesn't it?"

I looked up at the beautiful moon, it was full tonight which made everything glow, like an underwater castle.

"It does. I admire the moon."

"Do you?"

"Yes."

"Why is that?"

"No matter how many scars the beautiful moon has, it still hides them and continues to look beautiful."

"That's a poetic way of saying it."

Knight then stood up and offered his hand, I didn't really know what to do so I took it.

Knight then led me to a hidden bench by the rose bushes and sat us there.

"Augh, this is the first night I've been able to relax. don't you say Alice?"

I laughed and agreed. This actually was the first night I was able to relax a little.

"This all feels like a dream, don't you think Knight?"

"Yeah. You only see this kind of scene in movies, especially this kind of scene. It's feel's like we're underwater."

"That's the beauty of this hill."

"It feel's like we're the only people in this world."

"It does."

Knight suddenly stood up the lifted me up and threatened to drop me in some flowers.

Knight smiled so sweetly, it just made my heart skip a beat.

"Put me down!"

"Or what?"

I was able to get lose from his grip then I playfully tackled him to the floor.

"Or that!"

"Oh yeah?"

Somehow Knight rolled over pinning me to the floor smiling like he won a big contest.

"No fair!"

We began to laugh then Knight lied right next to me and we both looked up at the starts and the bats flying around.

"I wish I could be a bat."

"Why?"

"Because I want to fly. I want to know how it feels like."

"Only if you knew…"

"Huh?"

"Nothing."

"That's not fair Knight! Tell me what you said!"

Knight suddenly sat up and looked at me.

"Alright, fine I'll tell you."

I quickly sat up and I was all ears.

"So what did you say?"

Knight looked at me and I suddenly felt like I was being mesmerized by his eyes.

Knight then leaned in and pressed his lips against mine, and this time, I was expecting it.

9.

To Trust Or Not To Trust

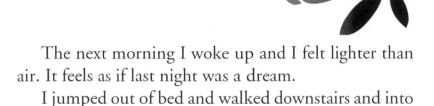

The next morning I woke up and I felt lighter than air. It feels as if last night was a dream.

I jumped out of bed and walked downstairs and into the kitchen.

"I should have a small snack and head back to my house, no matter what Knight and Jenny say."

I grabbed a juice box then left the kitchen.

"Good morning Alice!"

I turned and saw a red Jenny. I'm guessing she knows what happened last night.

"S-So how'd it go last night with Master Knight?"

"You know…"

"Eh?! Why would I know?!"

"Call it a sixth sense…"

Or the fact that your easier to read than an open book.

"You can tell huh?"

"yup."

Jenny let out a sigh and leaned against the wall.

"I wish I had your life Alice."

"My life? Why?"

"Your human, you can go outside and hang with friends. I mean, I can go outside, but I can't make friends like you do."

"Yes you can."

"How can I make friends? None of them will know about--"

"Then what am I? I know your secret, and it's not like I'll reject you."

Jenny let out a huge grin and hugged me tightly, I think I saw my life flash before my eyes.

"You know? In many ways, I would have never guess that you, a perky, hyper girl, would be a vampire."

"I guess not-- oh wait!"

Just then Jenny let me go and ran out of the kitchen.

The a few seconds later, she came back.

"Look!"

Jenny pulled out some clothes that were very bright.

"What are these clothes for?"

"Well, I have some money, so I decided to go buy some new clothes."

"For what? Are you guys going to a party?"

"No, I thought off a plan."

"Oooh. Jenny thought of a plan. Me like. So what's the plan?"

"Well since are biggest clue to what happened to your friends are them themselves right?"

"Right."

"So starting tomorrow, Wednesday, I will start going to school with you. Me and you will work together to figure thing's out."

"I like it."

A loud bell rang through the house.

"That means I should set up Master Knight's snack."

I let Jenny go and I wondered off.

Jenny's plan is good, and I need her to help me find out who exactly is behind all this.

If I was right all along and Creepsville is being brainwashed I want to find out who is behind it, and if it really is Knight.

Just making a theory of Knight being behind this made my stomach lurch.

"I guess it's time for me to look around…"

I wondered around through countless hall's, I think this maybe some sort of witch house.

When does it end and where does it begin?

"Master Knight?"

I duct behind a wall and watch Jenny go into a room. She was holding a metal tray with a vial with red liquid in it.

A chill went down my spine.

"Here's what you requested."

"Thank you Jenny."

So that's Knight's room, found it.

"Will that be all?"

"Yes."

Jenny left and Knight closed the door. If he's a vampire then he should be sleeping right?

Well… he's in some ways human too. He got hungry in the middle of his sleep.

"Let's wait just five more minutes then let him go back to sleep."

I waited and waited… and waited. I never knew five minutes felt like forever!

"Come on come on."

Six, five, four, three, two, one.

Time to go in.

"Quietly now…"

I opened the door as I quietly could and snuck in. This must be the room Knight is using for now.

It was plain looking actually, a white bed, sea blue curtains and carpet. A dresser, with a mirror even… but no sight of Knight.

"Damn… I if I were a vampire trying to sleep where would I sleep?"

I leaned against a wall, suddenly the floor opened and fell.

"I better not have a broken tail bone or else I'll--"

There it was… a coffin!

Knight's real bed…

"No way…"

I slowly inched towards it, but my legs were paralyzed by this discovery.

I leaned in on the lid of the coffin, and out my ear on the lid. I could hear breathing... it was faint, but it was there.

Knight's in there.

"Crap. If he comes out he'll see me for sure."

I looked around and see nothing but a bunch of bags and some dirt surrounding the coffin.

I look around till I see the opening of the trap door.

I quickly climb up the stairs and close the little trap door.

"I think this incident took some years off my life..."

I was about to leave when I tripped over a... painting.

"Knight and... another Knight?"

There was a painted portrait of Knight and a look a like... maybe his twin?

"Oh right! I have to get out of here."

I put the painting back and quietly slipped out of the room.

"There you are Alice!"

"Hey Jenny."

"Why so glum?"

"No reason."

Was I imagining it or did I actually see a painting with two Knight's?

"Hey Jenny, tell me something."

"What is it Alice?"

"Does Knight have some sort of brother?"

The look on Jenny's face was the look of horror. It went pale and her eyes looked dead.

She looked like a frightened child.

"Why w-would you think that?"

"Is that a yes or a no?"

Jenny quickly turned away and just started walking.

"Master Knight has never mentioned anything about a brother."

Look's like I'm not getting any answers from her, and I can't ask the source it's self, he'd get suspicious.

"More snooping I'm guessing…"

I walked down the hall and was about to go upstairs to Knight's room, but something caught my eye.

"Why are the light's on in the study?"

I looked around for any sign of Knight or Jenny. None.

"One peek wouldn't hurt right? Plus, if there's any info for detective Alice to scoop up, I'm there!"

I trudge towards the lit room, and open it swiftly and quietly.

I could be a ninja.

"Hello? Jenny… Knight?"

I turned to leave, but I suddenly felt a presence. I turned and saw Knight's back.

He was standing in front of the window by the desk.

"Oh, your awake. Jenny said you were sleeping. Are you all rested Knight?"

He just stood there, silently. I looked at the grandfather clock on the other side of the room.

It's barely five thirty, and outside was bright orange, the sun is still out… so why is he up?

"Knight? Are you okay…?"

The presence I feel is different from Knight.

"Knight?"

The man turned and his face was covered with a mask. It only covered his eyes, but his smile… it was so eerie…

"Alice… hello."

"Wait a minute, your not…"

My head… it feel's like it about to split open.

"Why would you make such a face when I'm here Alice? You love me don't you?"

I feel sick…

"Why don't you love me Alice?"

His voice makes me… so sick…

"Your not--"

"Alice… come here."

The stranger extended his hand to me, but I tried to back away, but the wall hit my back.

"Come here Alice…"

I tried covering my ears but his voice kept creeping into my brain and it made me get the worst headaches in history.

"Leave me alone!"

I closed my eyes, wishing that this would all go away.

"I love you Alice, do you love me?"

"No… leave…"

I opened my eyes and the black and white striped room was becoming blurry.

"Alice…"

"You not Knight! Leave now!"

I heard loud stomping noises down the hall.

"Alice?!"

"Jenny!"

I tried getting to the door, but my legs felt wobbly and I couldn't move, and before Jenny could get in, the door slammed shut on it's own.

"Who are you…?"

The window behind him shattered and he grew large, black bat wings.

"Until next time, my dear princess."

The Knight look alike then jumped out of the window and disappeared.

I quickly crawled to the door and opened it. Jenny came in and held me.

"Are you okay?!"

"I feel sick…"

"Umm right!"

Jenny then lifted me and took me upstairs in record time. She then gently placed me on the bed then went and brought me some medicine.

"Here you go."

"Thanks…"

"What happened? I heard you yelling, so when I came to check up on you the door suddenly closed and I could no longer open it."

I inhaled then exhaled, then explained everything to Jenny.

With every word she became paler and paler. For a minute I thought she would actually turn white.

"I see, well rest Alice. I'll go tell Master Knight about the what happened."

I nodded and let Jenny go, I feel to sick.

Alex said this before. He said a man was talking to him and it made him feel sick just by hearing talk. I never expected it to be that brutal.

"Augh, this medicine tastes awful... I need more water."

I slowly jumped out of bed and carefully went down the stairs, afraid that I'll fall because of what happened.

"HE WHAT?!"

"Master Knight, please calm yourself."

"I'm going to kill him!"

Knight and Jenny... she must have told him.

"Please think this through Master Knight, if he made a move before you could then that must mean he's got something up his sleeve."

"You right."

I could feel Knight's murderous aura, he must be pissed.

"I hate him..."

Knight suddenly started to kick the wall and Jenny was fussing over him.

Who ever that guy was, he was bad news.

"Master Knight I-"

"Where is she?"

"Excuse me?"

"Alice."

Crap.

"She's upstairs, resting, but Master Knight--"

"Wake her."

"Yes sir."

Upstairs, quick!

"Crap!"

I finally got back in Knight' room and hopped into bed quickly before Jenny could come in.

"Alice?"

"Yes?"

"Master Knight requests your audience."

"Umm, sure."

I get up and walk down to where Knight is. His face was that of a devil.

"You wanted to talk to me?"

"Yes."

I sat on couch across from Knight, and the air was heavy.

"So…"

"Your not going to school anymore."

"What?"

"Did you not hear me?"

"Your not my father!"

"It doesn't matter! Until we catch that--guy you are not to leave this house!"

Knight's voice rose and I was afraid to move.

"Your not my guardian…"

"Just listen to me Alice."

Knight's glowed red, and I knew that was a bad sign, knowing that he was indeed a vampire.

"Fine."

I stood up and stormed off. If he expects me to stay locked up in this place then he's wrong.

If that creep is connected to what happened to my friends and this town then you bet I'm up for the danger.

"Miss Alice!"

"Jenny!"

Wait-- did she say 'Miss'?

"Master Knight wasn't to harsh on you was he?"

"Why are you being so polite now Jenny? That's irritating."

"Oh I'm sorry--"

"Don't you dare say your sorry."

"R-Right."

"Any ways. What was it that you were asking?"

"Oh, right. I was asking if Master Knight went hard on you."

"Somewhat. He said I can't go to school anymore and he tried to mind control me I'm guessing."

"Mind control?"

"His eyes glowed red."

"He must be… hungry."

A chill went up my spine because of the way she said it.

"So Alice. What will happen now?"

"That's right. Our plan."

"I thought it would be perfect, because Master Knight wouldn't be at school because his energy is being drained just by staying out during the day, so I thought this would work but then *he* had to go and ruin it. Usually Master Knight is powerful enough and there's a barrier around the house so no one could get in, but I guess he's been weakening."

"So that's why whenever I'm attacked I'm brought here..."

Jenny nodded silently and I knew she was hiding more information.

"Jenny, I'm your friend right?"

"Yes!"

"Then why are you hiding things from me?"

"What do you mean?"

"You make the most obvious faces! Your easier to read than an open book. I know when your lying to me."

Jenny let out a sigh and nodded.

"Okay. I need to go give Master Knight some vitamins and his snack, go to my room and I'll meet you there."

"Got it."

I quietly walked down the hall then into Jenny's room. Her room still looked like a Gothic library.

"There's a bunch of books on the floor and some magazines on the bed. You ever wonder how this girl sleeps?"

I heard a little meow and jingling bells.

"Augustine!"

Augustine jumped in my lap and I noticed that she was finally healed.

"Are you all better Augustine?"

Augustine meowed a reply and snuggled in my lap.

"I missed you too."

The door suddenly flew open then slammed shut.

"Sorry Alice, Master Knight is brooding."

"No problem, so start explaining."

"Oh, right."

Jenny walked over to, what looks like, a desk covered in books.

She the pushed off books off her desk and pulled out a rolling chair.

"Sorry about the mess. Anyways, what is that you want to know?"

"Everything. Why is everyone here being brainwashed into goody-two shoes, why are my friends suddenly forgetting me, why are they after me?"

Jenny looked down at the floor then looked back at me.

"Knight's brother."

"His brother?"

"Yes. Remember you asked me if he had a brother?"

"Yeah…"

"Well he does have one, an identical twin brother."

"Twins? Is that why there were two Knight's in the painting?"

"Painting?"

"Never mind, go on!"

"Umm well it all started when they were young. Master Knight was always naturally smart and talented. By the age of six he was able to sprout wings and fly. His brother was almost equally talented."

"Almost? What's that supposed to mean?"

"He was always a step behind Master Knight. A lot of people praised Master Knight but he never cared. Master Knight's brother grew jealous and angry. Jealous that he never got as much praise as his brother and angry because Master Knight cared so little for the talent he had. By the time the two were thirteen Master Knight's brother grew enormously jealous and so one day he decided to put a curse on his twin brother."

"A curse? On Knight?"

Jenny nodded and looked at the red and orange curtain covering her large window.

"He placed a large tattoo on Master Knight's back. The tattoo was in the shape of black feathery wings with white cursive lettering on them. Knight could never fly into the night anymore, and if he did not get rid of the curse by the time he turns twenty, his life will be over, so over the years he's been losing energy because of that curse…"

I swallowed hard, almost afraid to speak… but I spoke.

"How would you cure it?"

"Many of the elder's have said to drink from his most loved maiden."

"Then we'll have him drink blood from me!"

"It's not that easy Alice. The problem is his feelings. He doesn't want you to suffer like he is... he wants you to be human."

I'd never thought about that...

"And what happened to Knight's brother?"

"On the night that he placed the curse on Master Knight, he disappeared... like a dream in a sea full of nightmares. We were finally able to track him down here, imagine our surprise when we found that this town was full of families who were unaware of the danger they were in, unaware that they were being controlled by a powerful vampire. What shocked us the most was you and your friends. You guys were the only ones who were untouched by the mind control waves, and we're grateful."

"But why am I the last of my friends. Why haven't I noticed this?"

"HE became aware of you guys when Master Knight came. He sent his goons after you, but Master Knight kept his eye on you with his bats."

"I see. Wait, why were we untouched by those mind control waves?"

"Your will."

My will?

"You said before that when you woke up from a nap you got the worst headaches correct?"

"Yes."

"Well, subconsciously you were battling them and the will to survive, the will of wanting to live helped you fight it, and without your help your friends would have surely lost their will to live and would have succumb to being mindless idiots and drones."

"Okay, I get that part, but why is he doing this?"

"To exact revenge on all those who have looked down on him. He wants to control an army of his own and take down the vampire society."

"What? Well can't the elder's or something stop this?!"

"That's a problem. A deadly miasma has leaked into our society. There's a king of the Vampire World, but he has become sick do to the miasma... and we just found out that it was Master Knight's brother who had released miasma upon us."

"That bastard..."

"I am only a half vampire, and Master Knight is losing his strength... even the rest of the vampire world refuse to go up against someone so cruel and powerful. He'll destroy us and rule the world..."

I finally stood up and rolled my hand into fists, digging my nails into my palm.

I couldn't believe that Knight had such a terrible brother!

"The vampire's won't stand up for them selves, but I'll stand up for humans and vampires."

"Alice..."

"If Knight's losing strength then we need to help him out ASAP!"

"How?"

"You know how to do barrier stuff right?"

"Yes, as a half vampire you need to learn at least the simplest things vampire can do."

"Then pack your things!"

"Eh?"

"Tomorrow morning we are going to school, but…"

"But what?"

"You better hope your barriers are powerful enough to protect my house."

"Wait-- you mean we'll be going to your house?!"

"Yup. I'm going to use myself as bait…"

"Alice that's dangerous!"

"Not if I have you."

Jenny let out a groan but I ignored it.

"So start packing Jenny. See ya!"

I walked over to the door and left with Augustine.

Halfway up the stairs I could hear down the hallway someone playing the violin.

It must be Knight…

Now that I know the story I can trust Knight.

10.

Is There Any Hope?

Morning finally arrived and I quickly got up.

It's five am. If I pack whatever clothes I have here and get Jenny in less than two minutes then we're good.

"You go to do what you got to do, right Augustine?"

Augustine meowed her reply and went back to sleep.

I heard a knock at the door and my heart pounded loudly. I hope it's not Knight.

"Alice?"

A female's voice… Jenny.

"Come in Jenny."

Jenny came in while I began to pack.

"Are you ready Jen?"

"Yup!"

I turned and expected to see her in her maid uniform, but instead I found her in normal clothes.

"Are those the clothes you showed me yesterday?"

"Yup. I fixed them up last night, don't they look wonderful?"

"Totally! I would actually wear them."

The bright clothes that Jenny showed me last night were now torn and had some bats and skulls stitched in.

Her pants had rips and tears, plus some safety pins.

"Do you need help Alice?"

"I'm good. These are the clothes that Knight lent me. I'm just going to wash them when we get to my house."

"Won't we be late?"

"For some reason the school called and there is a two hour delay."

"Yay!"

I finished packing, and now I'm ready.

"Would you like me to carry those Alice?"

"Sure, I'll grab Augustine."

I grabbed Augustine and suddenly she groweled and hissed.

"What's wrong?"

"I don't know. Augustine has never acted this way."

"We should go before Master Knight hears all this racket."

"Right."

We grabbed everything then left.

Finally arriving I felt calm, but Augustine was still acting up.

I placed her in my room where she kept running back and forth and jumping around.

"So this is your house huh?"

"It's mine completely actually. My parents left for over sea's, but every month they wire me money so I'm pretty much renting this place. The mansion my parent's own is way too big and scary. I don't really like being alone in huge places."

"It does get lonely. I remember one time I was sent to watch over Master Knight when he went to sleep over at the Vampire king's castle, and I got lost... I was so alone."

"Why were you guys sleeping over at Vampire King's castle?"

"Master Knight is a descendent of the Vampire King and one of the nominee's to be the next King of Vampires."

Whoa, that's a heavy role to fill.

"I'm going to take a shower now. Why don't you go ahead and set you stuff up in the guest room and do what you got to do."

"Roger that!"

I go upstairs and quickly undress and turn on the water.

It felt nice to take a shower in my own house again.

"Oww, too hot."

After stabilizing the water I get in and rinse and repeat.

I get out then brush my teeth and dry my hair then apply make-up.

Same old routine…

"Let's see… what to wear…"

I go through my closet and find and black plain skirt that has some random staples on them and a hot pink shirt with black vines and black roses.

I got dressed and met Jenny downstairs that was cooking something.

"I just love your kitchen Alice! It's not that big and it's not that small. It's just right!"

"Well I'm glad you like it."

I sat at the table and looked out the window where Knight once stood in front of.

I miss my dark prince… but this if for his own good. That curse of his will only suck away his life.

"Here you go Alice."

"What you make?"

"Just eggs with bacon."

"Smells good. I haven't had a real breakfast in a while."

For the first time in a while I had a nice conversation and a nice breakfast with a friend.

"What time is it?"

"Oh… right, it's up on the wall behind you."

The time was eight fifty, time to go.

"Well, shall we get going?"

"Yup."

We get our bags and head towards to Jenny's car, the car that will take us to every teens worst nightmare… school.

"Here we are."

"Unfortunately…"

"Oh Alice, be more happy?"

"How?"

I didn't notice but I just realized how miserable I am right now coming to school.

I was happy to skip out on a couple of days because of Alex and Anne and finding out that the entire Creepsville town is being brainwashed.

"How can you not be excited!"

"My question is why are you excited about to school?"

"Well this is the first time being in an actual school!"

"Oh… that's right. I forgot."

"Where's the office? I need to go register!"

"Just enter those doors and you'll see it on your left--hey! Wait till I'm done explaining!"

Jenny just took off, I guess she's really excited for school.

"Oh my god, is she actually here?"

"I thought she would have dropped out already."

"I heard that her friends finally abandoned her and she scared off that hot new guy."

"Really? She the worst!"

Ignore them… it's not really them. It's a vampire that is controlling them.

Inhale… exhale…

"So you finally show up for school."

I turn and see Anne and a new group of blonde chicks… cheerleaders maybe?

"Anne?"

"Humph. You have no right to talk to me directly freak."

Ouch… those words stung.

"Anne… what happened to you?"

"Hey, she said not to talk to her directly!"

My heart feels like it going to burst from all this pain…

I feel like I'm shrinking back into a helpless child…

"Alice! I'm in! I didn't think it was that easy!"

"That's good Jenny."

"Who are you?"

"My name is Jenny and I'm new here. Who are you?"

Jenny looks like she's ready to kill, you can sense it in her voice.

"Are you another friend of this freak?"

"Anne…"

Jenny immediately picked up on the situation. She grabbed me and held me close to her.

"Sorry Anne, but Alice is mine. She my best friend now."

"Oh? So you're a friend of that girl? Pathetic."

Jenny let me go and grabbed one of the other girls by the collar, almost lifting them off the ground.

"And you're a friend of this… *thing*? How pathetic, being friends with someone who does whatever mommy and daddy want."

Jenny let go of the girl and hugged me again, and this time she was back into her old air headed self.

"Come on Alice! Show me where this class is!"

"Sure."

I quickly glanced at Anne who's face looked cold, but her eyes looked really sad.

I followed Jenny into the school and showed her around.

"So where do you normally eat Alice?"

"In the abandoned hall."

"There's an abandoned hall here?"

"Yup."

I explained everything to jenny and she looked like a child learning something new.

"Sounds fun. I can't wait then!"

"Well... your going to have to wait."

The bell rang and I slowly turned to go back to class when Jenny stopped me.

"Wait Alice. Here."

Jenny handed me a bat shaped pendant and she held up a black heart.

"These are trackers that I created last night. If your in trouble just click the bat's tummy and mine beeps. It works vice versa."

"Wait... how will I know where you are or if you know where I am."

"Look."

She flipped over the my pendant and hers to reveal a small locater.

"This will tell right away where you location is."

"Sweet."

Pinned on the little bat and felt proud. I felt like some agent of the CIA or the FBI.

"Good evening Miss Parks. I see you have finally showed up to school, and with a new friend."

"Good morning Miss... umm."

I wish I would throw in the effort to remember their names a bit more.

"Blithe Miss Parks! It's Mrs. Blithe!"

"Sorry, sorry."

Mrs. Blithe is a tall scrawny looking woman... sometimes I wondered is she was a bird woman with weird clothes and glasses.

"So who are you?"

Jenny pulled out her paper's and handed them to her.

"I see. A new student, well then, I welcome you Miss Katherine."

"Thank you."

The bird woman walked off without so much as another 'humph' towards me. I don't know if I should call that rude or another less annoyance.

"He knows."

"What was that Jenny?"

Jenny's face was dark... like Knight's.

"*HE* knows that Master Knight and I are in town."

"How can you tell?"

"Mrs. Blithe seemed really tense just now."

"Are sure it's not because of me?"

"I'm quite sure."

"Well... she is nice with new students..."

"Exactly. She's tense with me."

So I guess our plan is almost spoiled. Maybe that's why Anne didn't recognize me at all.

"Well let's get you to class Jenny."

"Roger!"

I don't think I can handle Jenny's random mood swings.

Class… the place where I met night and the place where I lots Anne…

"Freak."

That's creative Anne.

"Students. If you don't mind calming down I would like to hand out papers."

The teacher handed out papers like it was any other day… but it's not.

"Nice of you to join us Alice Parks."

"Yeah… nice."

"Why don't you--"

Mr. Stickman's hand started to twitch and he obviously was panicking.

I could hear him whispering some words, then a minute later his hand whipped across my face, by the time I knew what was going on I was on the floor.

"OH! I'm so sorry."

Mr. Stickman quickly rushed over to help me up, which is odd because he had never shown any sign of kindness towards me or anyone else.

"It's fine Mr. Stickman. I can get up just fine."

As soon as Mr. Stickman helped me up he immediately snapped his hand back as if I were a disease.

"Please go to the nurse to go check on that scratch on your face."

"Yes sir."

I immediately grabbed my things and left before any of the students can either start gossiping or laughing at me.

At the nurses office I waited for five seconds then left.

No way I'm staying here.

"Now, to go tell Jenny what happened."

Halfway across the campus I heard someone talking, to someone or maybe to… themselves?

"I can't do this anymore!"

I sneak in closer to see who and who are talking.

"I hit a student today! A STUDENT!"

Mr. Stickman? What's he doing?

"Augh! Please! My head… I don't feel well… please."

Mr. Stickman was almost in a cradle position… just like Anne when I showed her the dress.

He looked like he was being tortured… like I was with Knight's brother.

"Mr. Stickman… are you okay?"

Mr. Stickman stopped his crying then got up and walked passed me.

I turned to see at least his back but he was already in the building… leaving me out here with questions racing through my head.

The bell had rung and I tried to find Jenny, but by the time I saw her the principle had grabbed me.

"Good evening Miss Parks."

"Umm hello… may I help you?"

"Humph, always with the remarks."

I have totally forgotten the principles name, but everyone calls her Principle No Heart. No Heart looks like a total beach beauty underneath her suit, but once you hear her nag, it ruins her image.

Her blonde hair and her D sized cups are the only things that help her survive in a men's world.

"To my office please."

I let out a sigh and followed her to a very familiar place.

"Please take a seat Miss Parks."

"Sure."

I sat down and already the office has noticed and me and start saying things.

"Idiots…"

No Heart came back in and signaled me to her office. After a couple minutes she came back in and sat down across from me.

"Again Miss Parks, why aren't you wearing appropriate clothing?"

"This is appropriate, it's just your tastes that aren't appropriate."

No Heart sighed, you could tell she was already losing her patience.

She looked over her papers and began to nag me. I decided not to pay much attention to her random naggings.

She hardly changes her office. Maybe it's because her mind is being controlled? I mean there's only white walls, a desk, and some diplomat stuff on the walls.

"Are you listening?"

"Huh?"

She let out a sigh and stood up and walked around, especially around her desk, a sure sign she has lost all patience.

"I said, you haven't been coming to school lately, I understand it's because your friends suddenly deciding to blend in and abandon you but please come to school."

She looked at me smirking, thinking she broke my wall down, but I already decided not care. I know their being controlled so I spent hours thinking it over and finally decided to make a wall protecting me from these feelings.

"Well that may be, but at least my friends were true to me, unlike the men you dated just to get in your pants-- excuse me, skirt Miss D cups."

No Heart's face got red with either anger or embarrassment, but either way it was funny.

"Now if you don't mind I really must go."

Before she could have a chance to say anything I ran out and out of the office. I could hear a faint scream and some crashing.

"Serves you right for hitting below the belt."

The campus was empty meaning class had already started.

"I guess I should get to class too…"

I decided to head to class and wait till lunch.

The lunch bell rang and I got out of class faster than any person would when you scream fire.

I passed countless glares and stares from classmates. When I arrived to A-hall's entry I saw Anne and Alex, plus their little gang.

Anne was hanging on Alex's arm, who was dressed in complete white, but when he saw me he immediately shook off Anne.

"Why if it isn't Little Alice."

My mouth was open in shock…

"Surprised to see me or something?"

"No… I'm surprised to see you and Alex together… I never would have thought."

Alec, Anne, and their little gang came closer to me and cornered my to the door in front of A-hall.

"Is this where you hang out during lunch?"

"Non of your business."

Anne came closer to my face and laughed. She looked up and laughed even harder.

"Maybe I should tell the teacher's about you eating here in this filth of a place. When they kick you out it will be easier to get you."

Anne finally pushed me through the doors, and before I fell I grabbed onto her pale hand.

I crashed through the doors, barely missing the fence that stopped you from getting into A-hall.

There was a one-foot distance between the door and the gates blocking off entrance.

Anne laughed and laughed, she laughed so loud and hard that it would echo through out A-hall.

"How pathetic."

Anne's friends laughed while Alex stayed in the back staring off into space.

"What do you do here? Feed the rats?"

Anne's little gang laughed even harder. Off in the distance I could hear wings flapping, and within seconds bats had swooped down, barely missing their heads.

I heard someone climb over the fence then a stomp next to me.

"No, correction. We're feeding our dear little friends... the bats."

"Jenny..."

Jenny lifted her hand and signaled the bats to just surround the gang till they left.

Jenny helped my up and I gave her a huge thank you hug.

"Thanks'."

"No prob. I just couldn't stand the loud laughter disturbing my familiars."

She signaled the bats back into A-hall.

"Come, those brats wasted half our lunch."

I nodded and climbed over the fence with Jenny.

I loved how Jenny could be very childish, but when the time is to be serious, she becomes scarier than any war hero.

"Here. I brought you some food."

"Thanks, but I would have been fine."

"Well you need to eat."

I nodded and accepted her food.

I sat down and began to eat, but then I stopped. Something was bothering... like something had happened to my hands. I outstretched my hand and kept looking it over.

"What's wrong Alice?"

"Nothing... it's just that my hand feel's weird."

"What do you mean?"

I flipped my hand over and over again until it hit me.

"Her skin..."

"Whose skin?"

"Anne's."

Jenny shrugged it off and gave food to the bats.

My hand felt weird because when Anne pushed me I grabbed onto her hand and it felt waxy.

Anne was conscious about her skin, so she always put some kind of lotion on. Anne's skin always felt soft... so why does it feel waxy now?

"Hey, Alice?"

"Yeah?"

"How do you think Master Knight is?"

"What do you mean?"

"I mean... don't you think Master Knight would have noticed by now that we're gone?"

"That's... true. He's not stupid..."

Jenny let out a sigh and looked up at the cloudy sky.

Her and Knight do the same thing...

"It's fine Jenny. If we don't hear anything from him by Friday then we'll go and check on him."

Jenny looked at me and gave me a not so sure smile.

"Okay."

I guess shouldn't tell her about Mr. Stickman...

"So how was your new day here?"

Jenny looked me and gave me an actual smile.

"It was wonderful, except for all the glares."

"Anything good happened?"

I doubt it, but it doesn't hurt to ask.

"Yes. There was a boy in my third period... he's nice and loves music."

"Really?"

Jenny nodded and smiled even bigger till it was a huge grin.

"I can sense that he hasn't been fully robbed of his conscious..."

The bell rang and I guess the conversation ended.

"Shall we get going?"

I smiled and nodded.

"Let's."

I guess there is hope for us here in this brainwashed town called Creepsville.

11.

The Nameless

Two days passed and me and Jenny have been doing pretty well. Jenny taught me some karate moves, just in case, but other than that nothing new has happened, but I'm still keeping my eye open.

Friday finally rolled in and no word form Knight.

"Morning Alice."

"Morning."

I jumped the last steps and sat at the kitchen table.

"Your ready early."

"I'm just a bit nervous today…"

Jenny nodded and agreed. She also looked a bit shaken… I guess the thought hasn't slipped her mind either.

"So do you want breakfast this morning?"

"No…"

"I thought so, so that's why I just skipped breakfast and made us lunch."

I smiled and got up.

"I'll go get your bag."

"Thanks Alice."

I went back upstairs and into Jenny's room and grabbed her bag. I looked around the walls of her room and saw nothing but posters of models.

I guess she actually wanted to become a model…

"Alice! Hurry if you want to get to school on time!"

"Coming!"

I ran down the stairs and almost slipping.

"You really are a bit of a klutz Alice."

"Am not."

I closed the door behind us and jenny grew her wings.

"You know… I'm kind of afraid of being caught…"

Jenny lifted me and smiled.

"It's fine. I promise you we won't get caught."

I laughed and when I opened my eyes we were in the air, on our way to school.

"You wonder why the back of the school is always deserted like this."

"Students either need to be in the cafeteria, library, or in classes before school starts."

Jenny started to go on and on about how stupid the schools rules are.

"Has any one seen the B-hall's teacher's?!"

"The principle disappeared too!"

Jenny and I carefully went within ear shot of the office and heard nothing but screaming, panicking staff.

"They just suddenly wondered off so suddenly ad never came back!"

The teachers started to run out of the office to try and look for the missing ones.

"Let's go Alice."

Jenny grabbed my hand and we ran all the way to A-hall.

This time we didn't climb the fence, we just stayed between the fence and wall.

Something in my heart began to quiver.

"What do you think is happening Jenny?"

"I can't say for sure… but it might have something to do with *Him*."

"Him?"

Jenny stared off to somewhere far away… and suddenly I felt frightened.

"Well, the bell will ring soon. Do you want to go to class?"

"Yeah. I think it would be good if both of us thought separately."

Jenny nodded then we both parted.

As soon as I realized Jenny was out of sight and earshot I decided to head back to the office.

The office was completely empty so I decided to take a small… peak.

I sneaked into the principles office and decided to see what's up.

"Let's see what you've been looking at in your desk."

While she called me into her office the other day she kept circling around her desk.

I opened up a drawer, but it was full of papers related to school. Then I tried to open her main drawer, but it was locked.

I grabbed a stapler on her desk and smashed the lock. The lock crumbled a little bit but it did not unlock.

I tried again and again until it finally broke off and opened.

I grabbed papers inside of it and spread it on the table she had in the corner for students.

I looked over the papers only to realize they weren't papers but maps!

I heard a knock at the door and I immediately looked up.

"Good morning Miss Parks."

"Principle… ma'am… good morning."

"What do you have there?"

No Heart's face is much more colder than usual… her eyes were piercing me…

"Do not make me repeat myself."

Why has No heart suddenly gotten more scarier?

"It's nothing, just some maps from class. I just came in here to talk to you."

No Heart suddenly lashed out and grabbed my neck, making me hit the wall.

"Stop lying girl…"

No Heart squeezed and squeezed I felt like I couldn't breath anymore.

I grabbed No Heart's hands and tried scratching her off, but her skin felt waxy and my hands kept slipping.

"There' s not way help will come to you."

The office started to flood with other teacher's and staff. No Heart let go and suddenly left.

I coughed and hacked then grabbed the maps and left before No Heart came back and finished me off.

I decided to ditch classes and went to A-hall. It was the only place that I could be safe from teachers and people.

"Let's see… if No Heart has the guts to attack me then that must mean that these maps are that important."

There were only four maps and two of them really looked old. Two of the maps belong to the neighboring town of ours.

It looked like one of the maps was the old version and the second one was a newer one. Same goes for ours I'm suspecting.

"But what is He looking for?"

As I was about to give up I saw one of Jenny's bats staring back at me.

I smiled and kept looking through the maps. If there is anything in here I will find it!

The bell rang signaling Lunch.

"I quit! I've looked over them over and over!"

I heard the fence cling and looked up to see Jenny.

"Hey Alice. You been here all day?"

"Yup."

Jenny looked at her familiar and it came to her, soon the rest came as well.

"So what did you make for lunch today?"

"Umm… well for you I made some paste with Alfredo sauce."

"Yum!"

We began to eat quietly till I noticed her looking at the maps then back at her food. It's cute how easy she is to read.

"Is there something you want ask Jenny?"

"Eh?1 Umm… well you see…"

"The maps?"

"Hah… umm yes."

"Heh, well I decided to go back to the office and look No Heart's desk."

"No Heart's?"

"Oh… that's right. You don't know."

I was about to explain everything but then a bat began circling above us making a weird noise.

Jenny called it to us and looked at it's eyes. After a minute or so she let it go and I could see that she was shaking.

"Jenny? What happened?"

Jenny turned to me and she looked like she was about to cry, but then smiled.

"Sorry about that, I just cut my finger and it hurts…"

"Is that so?"

What is she not telling me now? Obviously something's wrong, but she's never been able to hide it this well.

"I forgot something at your house, I'll go get it. If I'm not back by the time school end go home."

"Go straight home?"

"Yes."

"Wait... but why?"

"Remember, your still in danger Alice."

The way Jenny is speaking to me it sounds like an order.

"Fine."

"Finish your lunch alright?"

I ignored Jenny till she left. There was no way I'm staying out of this if it involves the last two people who are sane here.

"But how am I going to find out where she's heading? I can't follow her, she'll find out."

Just then, I spotted a bat. One of Jenny's no doubt's.

"Hey Mr. Bat... come here for a second."

The bat came flying down and landed on a branch near my head. I immediately took out some sort of food to bribe it with.

"I'll give you jerky if you show me where Jenny went."

For a minute there was nothing but silence between the bat and I, then it squeaked then took the jerky.

"So your going to show me?"

It flew circles above me, I guess it was a yes then.

"Alright, show me!"

It then flew off and I chased after it as if it were my only string of hope in this dark world.

Jenny's familiar led me up the hill leading to Knight's house.

My heart ached... remembering Knight and not being with him made it so much lonelier.

I wonder though... what is Jenny doing here at Knight's place?

"Alright... I'm guessing the front door is out of the question..."

The familiar then led me to the back of the mansion, where everything looked destroyed.

Panic started to overcome me and my leg's started to run on their own into the house.

Once in the house I stopped and started to breath again.

"Jenny? Knight?"

I walked down the hallway into some unknown room that looked like it belonged to Knight's parent's.

I then went down another hall and finally found my self in a familiar looking dining room.

"This house could become a Labyrinth if it wanted to."

I went through the kitchen and when I saw the main entrance of the mansion I felt sick.

The main entrance was almost completely destroyed. The walls looked like they are about to collapse, and vases were smashed everywhere. Some of the railing from the stars were spread around, paintings were stepped on and smashed.

I slowly began to go up the stairs, and little by little I saw blood. Every step had it's own little drops of blood each.

"Knight? Jenny? Come on guy's, answer me!"

I slowly climb up the stairs, and with each step brought fear…

I dreaded going back into the study room, so I head for Knight's room.

I thought Knight would be in his room healing or something, but when I opened the door to his room he wasn't there.

Everything was neat and untouched.

"I guess he's not here…"

I let out a sigh and turn to leave, not even bothering to close the door, when--

"Oh my dear Alice… How thoughtful of you to come visit me."

I turn to see Knight's brother.

My mind is going blank and right now my leg's feel really weak, I can't run…

"What's wrong Alice? You look like a frightened rabbit."

Every time he opened his mouth and words came out I felt sicker and sicker.

"Come here my sweet."

He outstretched his hand to me but I refused and instead I tried to run, but my leg's would only wobble so much down a hall.

Knight's brother was able to catch up in no time.

He then pulled my hair so hard I fell back.

"Why are you doing this?"

He just chuckled and pulled my up to my feet by my hair. My head was screaming in pain.

"One reason... hate."

"Hate?"

He then dropped me on the floor then lifted me over his shoulder like I was nothing but a sack of potatoes.

"I bet you Knight or Jenny have told you my name."

That's true... those two never told me his name, they just called him *Master's brother* or *Him*.

"Would you like to know Alice?"

Before I could answer... I passed out.

When I awoke I was a large white room with cords all over me.

I tried to move but I was strapped in like a mental patient.

I looked around and saw other beds with people strapped in them with cords coming out of their arm's.

"Hello?"

They didn't move, I'm guessing help is out of the question...

"Is someone else awake?!"

I tried to look up to see whoever was talking.

"Excuse me! Is someone else awake?"

I gave up on looking and decided to just talk to the person.

"Yeah I'm up. Where are we?"

"Fantastic! Another person to talk to."

Whoever was talking had a very raspy voice, meaning they hadn't had any for of liquid or have been yelling to much.

"Wait… what was the question you asked?"

And apparently their not that bright.

"Where are we?"

"Oh, to be honest I have no idea."

"Great…"

"All I know is that we're being kept in here for blood."

"Blood?"

I looked around and noticed that some of the tubes led to a bag filled with maybe a pint of their blood.

"Yup. For some reason someone has kidnapped us for blood."

Well the answer is obvious isn't it?

"Um excuse me."

"Yes?"

"What's your name?"

"My name is Alice, and yours?"

"Alice?! It's me Anne."

"Anne?!"

"Yes?"

No way… it couldn't be…

Anne had turned into another Creepsville snobby teen. The Anne I knew had been lost to brainwashing vampires!

"What are you doing here Alice?!"

"That's what I want to know! What are you doing here Anne?"

"Remember the day Knight came? After school you decided to walk and we took the car, and on our way home someone rammed into us, then all of a sudden I awoke here in this place."

"Really? Where's Alex?!"

"He's right next to me."

"Alright, stay put Anne. I'll get us out."

Anne suddenly went quiet, so I took that as a sign of waiting.

I quickly went to think about how to get out of these straps.

In my forearm there was a needle, I decided that this will have to do.

I stretched my hand far enough to pull out the needle, and once the needle was out I took a minute to swallow my scream of pain. Then I was able to wriggle my arm through the straps.

"Alice?"

"Yeah?"

I picked at the lock that held down my arms and my torso.

"What's happening? What's going on with this town?"

"I'll explain everything later, okay?"

Anne went silent again and the unlock came undone.

I was finally able to unbuckle the strap on my chest and become free.

"Did you get it Alice?"

"yup!"

I quickly got up, only to find out that I felt dizzy from the lack of blood.

"Are you okay Alice?"

"Yeah…"

I looked around for Anne and Alex, and it disturbed to see so many people I knew here.

Some of these people were kids from school, except some of them looked different.

"Alice!"

"Coming!"

I wobbled over to Anne, and I was happy to see she wasn't that sickly looking.

She was a bit pale and her lips were dry but she looked fine, no bite marks on the neck, no new fangs, no nothing.

I looked at Anne then at Alex. They were wearing the same outfits they were wearing last time I actually saw them.

"Alright Anne, I'm about to rip-- err take out the needle in your forearm okay? It'll only hurt for a second."

Anne looked like she was about to cry but she swallowed her fear and looked at the ceiling.

I carefully held down her shoulder then pulled out the needle.

"Now did that hurt?"

Anne looked at me with wide eyes.

"Yes it did! Your lucky I didn't cry."

"Yeah, yeah."

I went over to Alex and did the same thing. Once he was unstrapped he suddenly woke up.

"Alex?"

"Alice? Oh this is another dream right?"

"No Alex… I'm actually here…"

I helped Alex up and gave him a huge hug. This was the real Alex, and the girl behind me is the real Anne.

I was so happy to see these two that I actually began to cry.

"Alice?"

"Alice are you okay?!"

Alex hugged me tight and then Anne joined in.

"I'm fine… I'm just so happy to see the real you again."

Alex and Anne suddenly looked at me weird and I felt so compelled to tell them the whole story, but I kept it in.

"What do you mean?"

"I'll explain everything later. Right now we need to get out of here."

We quickly got up and walked over to the only white door.

Alex tried opening it but it was locked.

"How are we going to get out Alice?!"

"Hold on."

I stomped my foot a bit then tensed then relaxed my leg muscles. Then with one swift kick the door came crashing down.

"When did you learn that Alice?!"

"Oh, a while ago."

We then began to run down a hallway way, until I realized what this place was.

This was an abandoned building that was to be demolished soon. This place is located right in the middle of Creepsville.

"Hey Anne, do you know this place?"

Anne suddenly stopped and looked around, as if she just barely noticed this place.

"Nope. I'm sorry."

I let out a sigh and tried to think of some plans when Alex came to the rescue.

"I know this place. This used to be an old toy factory. Three of the four main buildings have been destroyed, don't know why this one hasn't."

"Do you know this place well? Like if there's any extra rooms are?"

"I know this is the second building, and there should be some kind of basement beneath this place. This second building was used for storage…"

I heard Anne squeal and then saw her pounce on Alex.

"Your so smart Alex!"

Anne suddenly stopped looking at me then turned surprisingly serious.

Suddenly my stomach was in knots.

"Why do you need to know where the basement is?"

Alex and Anne looked at me seriously, so serious it scared me.

"I said I'd explain it later didn't I?"

"Anne's right Alice. We want to know the truth, and that means right now."

Before I could think of an excuse, footsteps were echoing just down the hall.

"No time, we need to hide!"

We quickly hid in a room nearby. As we waited for the people to pass I heard Anne let out a small squeal.

Then I heard Alex let out a grunt. I turned to see what these two were freaking out about, and what I saw sent a chill down my spine.

"Oh my…"

Bags… hundreds of bags of blood, all filed by blood type.

The room was cold, so this was why.

"Alice… I'm scared…"

Anne hid behind me and Alex looked pale.

"So all of those people, me and Anne… we were all hooked up and strapped in for our blood?"

Alex turned to me, his face looked confused and in pain. I looked away… I couldn't look at him straight in the face right now…

"We should leave--now. We need to go down to the basement and help--"

"No!"

Anne suddenly ran to Alex and both of them looked at me with such a strange expression, all of a sudden I feel guilty.

"Alice…"

I covered my ears and ran out. I didn't want to hear their words full of doubt towards me.

"Why won't you tell us Alice?"

I tried my best to face them, but my body was frozen solid. I didn't want to face them.

"Yes Alice, why don't you tell them?"

Anne, Alex, and I looked around the halls for the disembodied voice till we saw the speaker.

"You… your Knight's brother right?!"

"Correct. Aren't you smart."

"Shut up! Where's Knight and Jenny?!"

"You can find that out on your own, but I do have a little proposal for you."

"And what would that be?"

"If you learn my name, then I might answer a few questions, but if you don't Jenny and Knight will die and don't worry, I'll give you a hint."

"That would be…?"

"My root's may be bad… but my leaves will always have a faint glow at night. Until you learn my name I shall remain Nameless."

Before I could interrogate him anymore he escaped…

12.

When Two Worlds Collide

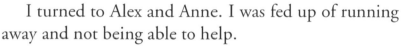

I turned to Alex and Anne. I was fed up of running away and not being able to help.

"Alex, I need you to tell me where the basement to this building is."

"Not until you tell--"

"Alex please! I'll explain everything to both of you later, right now lives are in stake!"

Alex stood there, thinking things over I'm guessing, then he motioned for me and Anne to follow.

We all rand down one hall and down another till we reached a room. Both me and Alex kicked down the door and looked around. The room was nothing more than an ordinary office.

"It's a dead end…"

"Not quite."

Alex moved a cabinet and revealed a hidden door.

"You're a genius Alex!"

After Anne gave him other compliments he looked at me and I smiled in appreciation.

"This is the basement."

"Thanks Alex, why don't you and Anne stay here."

I didn't want to involve Anne and Alex anymore than what they were. I don't want to see them get hurt.

"No way Alice! You've kept enough secrets from me And Alex! I wanna go to!"

Anne suddenly throwing a huge fit, and before I could reject the idea Alex grabbed my hand and looked at me pleadingly.

It's not fair… I just can't with these two.

"Fine, but when I say run you two run, got it?"

"Yes ma'am."

"Sure."

After agreeing on some rules we finally went down the stairs.

When we finally reached ground again Alex turned on the light's. It was amazing what was underground here!

At first glance it looks like this room is stacked with crates and boxes, but upon closer inspection you could see a whole row of block cells… like in prison's.

"Shugoi!"

Anne suddenly ran down the row of cells looking through each one, while me and Alex walked behind her.

"So what are you looking for Alice?"

"You should be asking 'who'."

"Alright, who?"

"Knight, and his maid, Jenny. Knight's brother kidnapped them and brought them here."

"So over the past few days we were gone you and Knight got chummy."

I stopped dead in my tracks. I looked at Alex as blankly as I could. I couldn't believe it! My best guy friend is accusing me of forgetting him and Anne!

"It's not like that!"

Alex came closer, till we were face to face.

"Then tell me, what kind of relationship do you have with Knight?"

Alex…?

"Alice! Alex! Come see this, quick!"

I started to run towards Anne, filled with relief to be out of that awkward conversation with him.

"What is it Anne?"

She pointed to a cell, and inside of it there was a person… a girl!

"Jenny!"

I run towards it and see a badly beaten up Jenny chained to the wall.

"Jenny…"

My eyes started to well up with tears, every cell inside of me was in a knot… fearing the worst.

"That's Jenny?"

I looked at Alex who looked at her with amazement.

"Who's Jenny, Alice?"

"She's Knight's maid… and my friend…"

Tears began to fall when Jenny finally came to.

"Jenny! Your live! Oh thank god!"

Jenny looked at me with a relieved look and a shocked look at the same time.

"Alice! Your okay as well!"

I nodded and held on tightly to the iron bars.

"Alice… you must leave."

"Why? I came here to get you and Knight out of here."

"Alice… you don't understand…"

"Well first let us get you out of here then you can make me understand!"

I stood up, still feeling shaky from the thought of Jenny being dead.

"Why don't you sit down Alice, I'll get Jenny out."

"Alex…"

Alex sat me down next to Anne. I looked on in amazement at how determined Alex looked… I've never seen this side of him before…

"Jenny, please scoot a bit to the side."

Jenny moved the best she could, then Alex kicked down the iron cell door.

"You did it!"

I practically pounced o Alex and gave him a big hug.

"What would I do without you?!"

I then let Alex go and ran to Jenny and unlocked her chain cuffs.

Alex and Anne then sat beside me and Jenny, and all the while I thought 'What's wrong Jen'?

"Alice… you and your friends have to get out of here."

"Why?"

"Because *He's* using half of the population of Creepsville for blood and the other half for war."

"What do you mean?"

"Master Knight's brother is brainwashing people, that way he can use them for war again the Vampire Society, but he's using half of the population for his own needs."

A chill went down my spine then back up.

"You mean… he's using them for food?"

Jenny looked grave, but I will not back down.

"Fine, if it's me, I don't mind, but Jenny… I need you to get Alex and Anne out of here."

Jenny looked at me as if stupidity has set in.

Anne began crying and we all looked at her.

"It's not fair Alice! I may not understand what your talking about right now but it sounds as if your sacrificing yourself for us! That's not fair, how come we don't have a say in this?!"

"Because…"

I helped Jenny up then helped Alex and Anne up and gave them a huge hug.

"Because I don't want you guys to get hurt anymore…"

I could feel everyone tense up a bit, but I held on to them tightly.

Alex suddenly broke loose form our group hug then pinched my cheek.

"Are you stupid Alice?"

"What?"

Alex let my cheek go, snapping it back into place.

"We'll get hurt even more if you die and we didn't help. I may not know Jenny well enough yet but I'm sure she wants to help as well."

I looked at Jenny and she smiled and nodded in agreement.

Before I could respond clapping echoed. We all turned to see who it was.

"Isn't this a touching moment."

"You…"

The man that was suddenly standing there was the same guy who tried to kidnap me a couple times.

"You're the creep who rammed us!"

"You're Michelle."

Jenny stepped in front of us, you could obviously tell she was limping.

"Miss Jenny… I haven't seen you since you were quite small, when was that, almost a decade ago?"

"There's no time for chit-chat, where's Master Knight?!"

"As you said, there is no time for chit-chat."

The man named 'Michelle' took out a whip and tried to strike Jenny with it. The minute it made a crack in the air fire illuminated the whole whip.

"Alice, I need you and your friends to leave, now!"

"But--"

"There's a door in the back, that's where Master Knight was taken. Do me a favor and find him, then you can come back for me."

Jenny looked at me smiling, she then looked back at Michelle and shooed me away.

"Fine, just promise me you'll at least stay alive."

"Fine."

I grabbed my friends hands and led them to the back. We ran and ran until we finally saw a door.

"There!"

The minute the door was in sight Alex and I rammed the door with our shoulders.

The door slammed open and for a minute I felt pretty proud and strong... then I felt pain in my shoulder.

"So who was that girl exactly Alice?"

After rubbing my shoulder I turned to my friends.

"I thought I told you. Jenny is Knight's maid and she's my friend."

We all began to walk, unfortunately, they didn't stop with the interrogation.

"So when did you guys meet?"

"It happened the day after you guys were kidnapped, I was also attacked. Michelle came out of nowhere and suddenly put a cloth over my mouth, before I passed out I saw Knight and when I woke up I was in his house. I got out of his bed and saw Jenny. I guess we just became friends."

"So you stayed over at Knight's house then?"

Anne sounded a bit too excited when she asked that question. She always the first one to find out if there's a new couple on the block.

"I guess, he made me stay there but every time I tried to go home someone attacked me and I ended back at Knight's house. So I thought that I should at least find out why these guys were after us."

I let out a sigh and just walked with Anne and Alex in toe. My head hurt, it was swelled up with questions of my own. Like Should I really get these two involved? Can I really help in any way? Can I tell Alex and Anne about Jenny and Knight? and most importantly Is Knight alright?

"So did you find out why?"

My feet froze, it was a reaction to the one question I dreaded answering.

Should I or should I not tell them about Knight and his brother?

"N-No, I tried but there wasn't anything…"

I'm sorry guys…

"Oh… well I'm sure that Knight will tell us right?"

"Right!"

Anne turns to face Alex and stops him in his tracks.

"What's wrong with you Alex? You haven't said one word since."

Alex looked spaced out. He looked at Anne then at me, then he just kept walking.

"Alex has been sort of out of it, don't you think Alice?"

My chest hurt for some reason. I ignored and just nodded.

After five minutes of walking, and thinking of ways to learn Knight's brother's name, something finally came to me.

"Do any of you guys know Romanian?"

Anne shot her hand up in the air like it was class.

"Oh! I do! I do! I do!"

"You do Anne?"

"Yup. Momma and Papa made me learn a whole bunch of foreign languages. Why do you ask?"

"Remember how that guy on the speaker said we had to learn his name?"

"You mean Knight's brother?"

"Yeah, you know how he said that we need to figure out his name in order to find Knight and Jenny?"

"Yeah?"

"Well I figured…"

Knight's brother was mysterious… he appeared and disappeared like the night. He was scary… and menacing like a nightmare… but his there was that tip he gave me. 'His roots may be bad but his leaves may have a faint glow at night'. What could it mean?

"Alice?"

"Could it be the flower--"

Just then footsteps echoed down the hall. Before we could even walk away who ever was coming down the hall saw us.

"You there! Stop!"

"Alice… what are we going to do?"

Anne clutched my sleeve and Alex just stood there, tensed up.

"I asked who you three are?"

The person questioning us came into the light and what I saw shocked me.

"Are you going to answer me?"

Anne recognized her right and hopped for joy.

"Momma!"

Anne was about to go and hug the woman who looked like her mother when I stopped her.

"Anne, stop! Think about it... why would your mother be in a place like this?"

Anne looked at me with a blank look then started to ponder what I just said.

Before Anne could answer me the woman who looked like her mother grabbed her shoulder gently.

"Anne darling... don't listen to your friend, listen to mommy. Mommy knows what's best."

The look-a-like woman stoked Anne's hair and gave Anne a hug.

"Let go of me!"

Anne pushed the look-a-like away and ran behind Alex.

"Anne darling--"

"Mother called me darling, she never talked to me that sweetly nor has she ever called Alice my friend!"

Miss look-a-like made a face like she had smelled something disgusting.

"You think you can mock me?!"

Miss look-a-like was about to strike us when another look-a-like stopped her.

"That's enough. *He* doesn't need anymore problems."

I could hear myself let out a little gasp as the look-a-like turned to me.

"So you're the person I'm supposed to replace? What a joke."

"There's two Alice's?"

The look-a-like of me turned to Anne and suddenly charged at Alex and Anne. She jumped in the air and then kicked Alex and Anne, sending them flying.

Luckily they hit the wall softly… if you could say that.

"Now it's your turn."

I backed up until I hit the wall. I looked around for anything to use as a weapon.

"No one can save you now."

The look-a-like looked at me with cold eyes. It was like she hated me with a passion.

"Why do you have to kill me?"

"Oh I won't be killing you darling, I won't be having the pleasure of doing that. My job is just to take you to my master."

"But--"

Look-a-like Alice slammed her hand onto my throat.

"Just shut up, stop talking! I don't want to hear that pathetic voice that my master loves so much!"

I could feel her hand quiver a bit, but before I could ask anything she gripped my hand and threw me across the hall, making me crash through the wall.

I coughed and coughed, trying to gain back air from that collision. I couldn't get up… it hurt as if my bones had turned to glass and have shattered.

"Suffer the pain I have Alice!"

Look-a-like Alice began to kick my stomach and she kicked harder than the last. I couldn't regain my breath fast enough and I was losing consciousness.

My mind began to go blank, the first thing I wanted to do was to yell for Knight but I can't do that… he can't save me.

"What is it Alice? Does it hurt?!"

I tried to block her kicks by curling up into a ball, but it was of no use. No I just have to rely on instinct.

I reached out for anything, anything to use as a weapon.

"Don't think so!"

Look-a-like Alice stopped on my hand. It hurt so much already and with her stomping it hurt twice as much.

"This is the last time you will ever be conscious."

"I don't think so!"

I heard a thump and the look-a-like Alice went to the floor grabbing her neck. I looked up to see who was my savior this time.

"Anne! Are you okay?!"

Anne helped me up and I hugged her tightly.

"Are you okay Alice? It looks like she did some damage."

"I'm fine she just gave me some bruises."

I looked behind her to see the huge hole in the wall that I had made. Then I looked at Alex.

"Is Alex--"

"He's fine, I took martial arts class so I can handle pain better than he can."

"That's good."

Me and Anne smiled at each other, but Anne suddenly stopped and looked fierce.

I turned to see what she was looking at and saw look-a-like Alice up and glaring.

"You think having your friend here will help you Alice?! You know something… your nothing more than a power hungry slut!"

"Don't you dare talk about Alice that way!"

"You think your all that Alice, but all you want is power for YOURSELF! That's why you have my master and his worthless brother wrapped around your pretty little finger."

Before I could think properly I lunged at her and punching her in the face. I pulled her up close to me till we were face to face.

"Don't you ever talk about Knight that way ever again!"

"It's true. You have the two most powerful vampires wrapped around your damn finger just so you could become a vampire and have power all for yourself!"

I slammed the look-a-like to the floor and got my fist ready to punch her, but for some reason tears came instead of that punch.

"I love Knight with all my heart! How dare you say that!"

Look-a-like pushed me off then pinned me to the floor.

"You are such a liar! You just want power for yourself! How you got my master to fall for you I will never know!"

She began to tremble then looked at me with hatred and sadness combined.

"It's not fair… I love him so much but I can never get him to look my way. He never looks at me unless it's to remind him of you… it's not fair…"

"You really love him…"

Look-a-like Alice snapped back into her furious self tightened her grip on my wrists to the point where it felt like they were about to be snapped off.

"I do, but it doesn't matter what I do for him he only wants you! Him and Knight! I can't believe they fell for someone as greedy as you!"

I found strength in my legs and Kicked her off and stood up, clinging to the wall for support.

"The only power I need is to protect the people I love, but I've gained that power from courage!"

The feeling of wanting to protect someone turns to courage and courage is what gives you power.

"Just shut already!"

I quickly turned to Anne who was still standing there. Her face was that of an undecided emotion.

"Anne I didn't mean to--"

"Look over here Alice!"

I turned to see look-a-like running towards me, and before I could dodge her, she jumped and kicked me in the stomach hard enough to send my flying across the room and crash through the wall once again into the dark night.

I coughed and coughed and tried to get air in but it hurt so much to just breath.

"Crap... I think I have some broken ribs..."

I clenched my teeth then stood up. A pain shot up from my left leg then another shot up from my left arm.

"Come on Alice, is that you got? Don't you want to protect your friends?"

I could see in look-a-like's hand she held Anne by her shirt and in the other Alex.

"Please don't hurt them!"

She just smirked and dropped them then came at me.

I dodged her first couple of hits and was able to get a couple of hits in. By the end of this small spar we were both out of breath. I never knew I was this fast dodging.

"Your good, but not good enough!"

In the blink of an eye the look-a-like took out six knives and was getting ready to throw them at me.

"W-Wait! I thought you said you can't kill me!"

"What my master won't know can't hurt him."

She through one knife and it missed me.

"Ha! You missed--"

My sentence was cut off short when a trickle of blood went down my face.

"Humph, I never miss!"

As she readied herself for another attack I ran, but I didn't even make it two feet when my body suddenly collapsed in pain.

"Poor thing, does it hurt?"

Look-a-like Alice stomped on my left arm again and again. I wanted to cry out but nothing came out.

When she finally stopped she held a knife to my throat, pressing it harder and harder until a drop of bloody trickled.

"This is the end. I'll become the real Alice and my master will love me!"

The only person who can stop her is--

"Stop or I'll call your master!"

"Your bluffing!"

"Try me."

A flower with roots that are bad but the leaves will always have a faint glow...

"Silver Sage!"

The look on the look-a-like's face was stricken with horror.

Bingo.

"What is it now?!"

A male's voice surrounded us, I looked around frantically but saw no one.

"Master…"

Once look-a-like got off my I carefully got up, making sure not to cause myself pain.

"No way… I actually got it."

Knight's brother… his name is Silver Sage.

"How are you Alice?"

I turned to see who had whispered in my ear and saw Knight's brother-- err, Silver Sage. He looked different than last time… his hair… it's glowing faintly.

"You seemed surprised, Alice."

I quickly backed away when I noticed that he was too close for comfort. There were so many things I wanted to do to him.

I wanted to strangle him for making me worry about my friends, and making me go through this hell, but then I wanted to question him first. I decided to just bite my lip and question on the where bouts' of Knight and Jenny.

"Is there something on your mind, Alice?"

I shot the most dirtiest look at Silver Sage. Obviously he didn't see it.

"Where's Knight and Jenny?"

Silver cocked his head to one side then the other, as if wondering to actually answer me.

"Jenny… who knows."

"That's not fair! We had a deal!"

Silver lifted his hand as if to stop me from talking.

"I said I didn't know where Jenny is. Remember that you and your friends let her go and she went off fighting with one of my guards."

"Then what about Knight?"

Silver looked me straight in the eye and gave me the most evil grin I had ever seen.

"He's safe for now."

"But where is he?!"

Silver pointed to the forest behind me. Smoky Forrest was a forest that was always covered with fog. Once you entered five feet in it you could hardly see your hand in front of your face.

Smoky Forest is like a border... between Creepsville and Senile city.

"In there?"

Silver nodded his head, his face filled with boredom.

"Now I told you where he is, now let's see if you can reach him before I do."

"That wasn't part of the--"

When I turned back to Silver he was already gone, along with the look-a-like Alice.

"Alice..."

"Alex!"

I quickly ran to Alex, making sure both him and Anne were okay.

"Alex, I'm so--"

"Some crazy crap we've gotten into, huh?"

"Yup. Some crazy crap..."

Alex looked at me kindly, then let out a heavy sigh.

"I'm really sorry for what I said back there... I don't really know what's going on but I'm sure Knight's butt's in trouble huh?"

I nodded my head in agreement. Then Alex sat up, wincing every two seconds.

"Don't sit up. Lay down for a bit, you might have bruised ribs."

Alex kindly removed my hand from his shoulder and pointed to the forest.

"Get going. Knight needs your help. I'm pretty bruised up and Anne is knocked out…"

I slowly got up, making sure that I didn't wince at the pain I had on my left side.

"Stay here then, take care of Anne."

Ignoring the pain I started off, running foolishly towards my death perhaps.

Ten minutes into the forest and I already couldn't see the tree's in front of me.

"Now I'm wishing it was day time, and maybe a sunny day would help out here too."

Finally after twenty minutes of running into tree after tree, after tree I could finally hear people talking.

Closer and closer I got till I could hear the muffled voices clearly.

"Your not going to fight me back Knight?"

"My order's were to bring you back… Alive dear brother."

Carefully, I looked form behind a tree, just to see Knight being beat up by his brother.

Silver raised his hand to hit Knight, and when I expected Knight to dodge it, he takes a brutal punch.

"Fight back! Stop sitting there!"

Silver took out a dagger and raised it to Knight's throat.

"Don't act calm Knight, you know if this dagger slits your throat it's all over. You haven't been drinking enough blood to keep up your strength, especially with that damn curse I put on you."

Knight sat quietly, his face was blank, but Silver was becoming furious with his silence.

"That's it Knight Aoi!"

"NO!"

After I had shouted my legs began to move and before I knew I was in front of Knight, suffering from a deep cut on my arm.

"Alice! What are--"

"Quiet Knight!"

My breath was becoming shallow and my body ached from pain, but if all this pain comes from protecting everyone then so be it.

"Why hello again Alice. You took longer than I expected."

"Sorry if I don't meet your expectations…"

Silver grinned for a minute then he stopped.

"Move Alice."

"No."

Silver yanked my hair and threw me like I was a rag doll. I tried to get up, but my body felt heavy… like I was chained.

"Knight…"

Knight looked feverish but he stood and tackled Silver to the ground.

"Don't you ever hurt Alice again! Do you hear me?!"

"I can do whatever I want to her! You don't deserve a girl like her!"

Silver lifted Knight like no big deal, and threw him ferociously against a tree, snapping the trunk.

"Knight… please be okay…"

I finally willed my body to get up. Tears began to fall because of the pain, but I was able to limp towards Knight.

More tears came, not because of the pain, but because of how badly Knight looked.

"Knight, are okay?"

"Yeah. Just get out of here okay? I'll meet you at the mansion--"

"Stop Knight! I know the whole story already. You need a cure and I have it, right?"

Knight's eyes widened a bit, but other wise they seemed feverish looking.

"Yes.. But--"

I exposed my neck and made Knight go closer to it.

"You have to Knight or else everything you fought for will be in vein…"

Knight's breath seemed to get a bit heavier, and he seemed to be losing consciousness but he seemed to be pondering it.

"No… Alice you have to--"

"Please Knight…"

I hugged Knight tightly, I heard Knight whisper something like 'Sorry' then I felt a little prick. He had finally bit into my neck. I could feel his fangs in my throat… sucking the warm, red liquid from my neck.

13.

The Ultimate Sacrifice

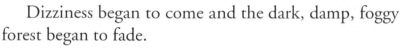

Dizziness began to come and the dark, damp, foggy forest began to fade.

I suddenly felt cold around my neck and before I could grab it, Knight had already placed me gently on the ground.

Before my vision began to get blurry, I looked at Knight. Knight had suddenly grown large bat like wings and was now looking healthier than before.

"That's good…"

"Please don't move Alice… I'm sorry."

Knight then turned towards Silver and began exchanging words, words that had become muffled and then my vision had went blurry… then the darkness settled in.

When I opened my eyes it was bright… the room was white and all was silent… until I heard Anne screaming…

"Everyone! Come quick! Alice is awake!"

I heard bustling voices and looked to my left.

"Hey there sleepy head…"

Alex, Anne, Jenny, and some student's from school were by my side. The student's from school who usually were in nothing but white clothing were now wearing nothing but colorful clothes. Each and every person was wearing things that showed off their personalities.

Some kids were wearing skinny jeans, other's were wearing regular jeans, and some girls were wearing some random skirts.

"What's going on here?"

A tall girl with brown hair and glasses stepped up and cleared her throat. She was wearing a private school type attire.

"Good evening Miss Alice. It's a relief to all of us to find you awake."

"Umm…thanks?"

"No, it is us who should be saying thank you."

As if on cue the entire class said 'Thank you'.

"For what?"

"Well for saving us of course. That maniac tried to lock all of us in that abandoned building and you tried to stop him. Honestly… I don't remember how on earth we managed to get stuck in there, but anyways thank you for saving us."

I gave them a smile then Anne pushed them out of the door.

"Alright everyone, I'm sure you want to see Alice right now, but me and Alex need to chat with our friends."

As soon as Anne shut the door questions came out of my mouth.

"What is she talking about?"

"Well, when we awoke Jenny was treating our wounds already and she had already filled most of the town's head with false memories, that way they don't question what they have been doing these past couple of years. Plus she explained the whole story to us."

"Oh. That's good."

A bit of guilt washed over me and Anne noticed.

"Kind of sad huh?"

"What is?"

"All these people are either full grown adults or in their teens and they have normal memories like we do. Their memories are made up.."

"That's true…"

Anne suddenly clapped her hands together and her face suddenly became bright.

"But that just means they don't have to feel bad right? Plus, they can always make new memories."

"Right…"

Anne chuckled a bit then glanced around the room then looked as if she were about to get ready to bounce from excitement.

"What's wrong Anne?"

"Nothing. Hey I just remembered something I have to do. Bye!"

Anne left faster than I could say Holy Bats.

"How are you Alice?"

"I'm doing fine. My leg and arm don't hurt as much."

"Well it shouldn't, you've been asleep for almost three weeks."

"Really? That long?!"

Alex nodded and smiled so sadly.

"What's wrong Alex?"

Alex leaned over and pressed his warm lips against my freezing pale ones.

The kiss felt like an eternity... but I realized that it had only lasted a couple of seconds when Alex pulled away.

We stood there looking at each other for a few seconds before either of us had spoken.

"Alex... I--"

"I'm sorry Alice!"

Alex then bolted out of the room before I could have any say in this situation.

I looked at the white sheets covering me... hoping that what had just happened was just a dream. Unfortunately, my daydreaming was ruined when a couple came in.

Tall slender looking woman with jet black hair. Her piercing brown eyes looked as if the could see right through you. She looked like a woman who was forty-five but looked like she was in her early thirties. Behind her was a man with black hair and had a small streak of white hair on the sides. He looked like an English man, his face had that mature look to it that made any girl swoon. His eyes were a light gray and he stood proud and tall, these two look perfect for each other.

"Alice!"

She knows me?

"Oh darling!"

The woman hugged me tightly and only then did I realized who these people were.

"Mom! Dad!"

I hugged my mother tightly then my father joined in.

"What are you guy's doing back in Creepsville?"

"To be honest darling, we don't know exactly what's going on. One minute I remember being pregnant with my soon to be baby girl then the next I'm out of some misty trance and find out that I'm in the middle France with your father, years have passed, and I had already given birth to you."

Mother began to get hysterical, so father stepped in to explain to me.

"It took us a while to track you, but we finally found you. You can imagine how shocked we were to see you already grown up."

My dad patted my head and he began to cry and for some reason I did too.

I wonder, did Jenny fill their head's with some fake memories?

"Dad I--"

"We know everything Alice. About Knight and…"

He trailed off and my heart sank yet it felt like dancing as well.

I didn't have to lie to them about what happened.

"You're a brave girl Alice… you made such a sacrifice…"

"Mr. and Mrs. Parks, Alice needs her rest now."

My mother father got up and left the room, but not before hugging me tightly and saying good-bye for the day. I couldn't help but feel sad, I only spent half an hour with them…

"Ms. Alice, we need to do a small check up on you, if you don't mind."

I nodded and the doctor examined me and said that he was surprised that I was healthy then left.

The doctor had reminded me of what my father had said to me-- I have made the ultimate sacrifice.

As long as I could remember I've always been out during the days with my friends. Under the cloudy sky eating ice cream with Alex and Anne.

I remember how I wished that one day I wanted to be out in the sun, just for a day, but now that Silver is gone his power's diminished and the sun is finally out… but I can't enjoy. The first time in my life I see the sun and I can only see it through cracks in the curtains.

I can't go out during the day with my friends to amusement parks, or have family fun days with my mother and father…

"I can only go out during the night I'm guessing…"

I slowly stood up and walked towards the curtains that kept this room dark. I slid my hand through the curtains and before I could touch the window I could feel my hand burn.

I quickly pulled it away and held my hand as if it were an injured baby.

Even though there was glass between my hand and the sunset it still burned.

I closed the curtains without getting burned again and sank to the floor. I held my knee's to my chest and waited in the dark for someone anyone to come and comfort me and show me how to survive my new life.

I closed my eyes and began to get drowsy.

Before I could let myself go to sleep I cried a little and whispered Knight's name, then went to sleep.

My eyes suddenly snapped open and I found myself back in bed.

I quickly looked at the clock that was hanging on the wall and saw that it was three thirteen.

"Are you awake Alice?"

I turned to the direction of the voice, and to my relief it was Knight.

Seeing Knight made me want to fly, so I immediately hopped out of bed and jumped into Knight's arms.

Knight immediately hugged me back and as he hugged my I could feel his muscles relax a bit.

"I'm glad you're here Knight!"

"And I'm glad that your safe and sound Alice."

Suddenly Knight pushed me away.

"Knight?"

"I'm sorry Alice I… I don't know what to do anymore. I want to hold you, but I'm afraid I'm going to hurt you like already have. I want to protect you with everything I have, yet I can't protect you from me. I--"

"Knight…"

I quickly grabbed his hand to calm him down. Then I gently touched his shoulder, and I could immediately tell he was beyond tense.

"It's okay Knight. The reason I let you was because I wanted you to feel better. Jenny told me about how that curse was sucking the life out of you, and if there was a chance I could help you I would."

Knight… I've never seen him this torn up before. He reminds of the first time we met. To me he seemed like a wounded child who kept things in to protect other's.

"Knight, look at me."

Knight looked at me and he looked as if he hadn't slept in centuries.

"You don't understand Alice, I don't want you to suffer like us. We can't experience the sun like humans could, We're constantly hunted by slayers, we can't survive without blood. Do you know what it's like to be treated like a monster?"

My heart ached, I didn't know vampire's were so misunderstood.

"I didn't want you to be in pain like us."

Knight walked past me and opened the curtains to reveal a full moon, glowing brightly as if to shine as much as it can for the first night of freedom.

Knight turned to me, with such a pained expression.

"Can you ever forgive me?"

My heart felt torn for some odd reason. Was it because Knight had turned me… or was it because I felt his pain and there was nothing I could say.

Finally I walked closer to Knight and caressed his jet black hair that reached down to his shoulder.

"Knight… I love you more than anything. I don't care that you turned me, what I care about is you. I love you so much I'm afraid that I'll lose you. So please… don't look at me that way."

For a moment it was silence between us. It felt like an eternity until he snaked his arms around my waist and held me close, and what seemed to be only minutes seemed like an eternity of happiness…

"You probably should rest Alice."

Knight then ended our long hug and I felt a bit sad.

"Why? I'm totally fine. The Doc said so."

"Still…"

"I'm fine. All my friends came to visit me and so did my parents…"

"Really?"

"Yup, I'm surprised."

"And why is that?"

"I never knew my mother was so bubbly."

Knight let out a chuckle, and I could feel the tension from before melt away.

I sat there wondering about his parents. How did they act? Did they act all noble or were they loving and caring? Did he have happy memories with his parent's as a child?

"What is it?"

"huh?"

"You seem to be staring at me Alice."

"Oh, it's nothing. I was just wondering."

Knight gave me a look of suspicion then shrugged it off.

"So your friends visited you as well huh?"

"Huh? Yeah…"

"Really…"

"What are you--"

Suddenly the image of Alex's lips pressed against mine flashed through my mind and I suddenly felt a bit meek.

"So I take it you know about Alex?"

Silence suddenly filled the air. I dared to take a looked at Knight's face, and it looked mad with jealousy.

I couldn't help but giggle a bit. Here was the most handsomest vampire ever who could have any girl but instead chose me, a human girl, and he was jealous over a human boy.

"What's so funny?"

"Nothing. You don't have to worry about Alex okay?"

I quickly gave a quick little kiss on the lips to show I wasn't lying.

Knight then ran his hand through his black hair, removing his bangs from his eyes.

"Well if he tries anything like that again I promise you someone will have a black eyes and there will be blood."

I couldn't help but feel a bit happy about his little jealousy tantrum.

"I guess it's time…"

Knight suddenly stood up and walked over to the curtain and covered it. That's when I noticed the sky turning a bit pinkish.

"It's already morning? No way!"

Knight quickly walked over to me in vampire speed and kissed me on the forehead.

"Get some rest. I hear tomorrow you'll be discharged form here."

He's right! I couldn't help but grin.

"Alright, but we must have a date soon."

Knight looked at me with longing eyes and for some reason… it made me feel a bit uneasy.

"Alright, I promise Okay?"

Knight then covered my in blankets and kissed my forehead once more.

"Get some rest my Alice."

"You too… my Knight."

He then turned off the light's and left, and right on command my body began to feel tired and so I let my body to lead my to sleep.

14.

Goodbye…?

It has been nearly a week since I was discharged from that hospital.

Now I'm out in the dead of night lurking around in the cemetery or hanging out at Anne's house.

I haven't really talked to Alex lately, but Anne tells me he's fine.

"So have you hung out with Knight lately?"

I turned to Anne who was reading "*Gothic Beauty*" on my bed, while I was getting dressed.

"Not at all, unfortunately…"

I let out a longing sigh then turned back to my wardrobe.

"But tonight we're going on a date and he'll finally meet my parents."

"Even though it's only been a week, don't you think that your parent's might embarrass you?"

Just the thought of that made my feet cold. The thought of Knight and my parent's meeting smacked me harder in the head than any baseball could.

"Oh bats your right! Anne, what am I going to do?!"

"Don't fret my dear, just try and act casual and make the meeting as short as possible."

"Got it!"

I then grabbed a beautiful strapless, black dress that had a beautiful lace underneath, and the design on the hem was of bats.

The dress looked almost Victorian except it reached to my knee's.

I quickly grabbed some fishnets and some black and white stockings.

I looked around frantically until I found my Victorian portrait neck lace and some bat shaped hair accessories.

"Anne do you mind helping me with my hair?"

Anne nearly jumped out of her Tripp pants that she was wearing.

"Of course!"

She put my hair up making it look like dangling black curls.

"You hair has grown longer Alice."

"I guess it has…"

After ten minutes Anne finally finished and she nearly screamed in delight.

"You look so beautiful! I wish I could take a picture!"

Anne suddenly looked a bit pale and I could understand why.

"Alice I…"

"No sweat love. No harm no fowl right?"

She nodded but I wasn't sure if she really got that it was fine.

"Why don't you pick some shoes to go great with this outfit.

"Okay!"

And with that she was back to her blonde, bubbly self.

After ten minutes of Anne making me try on shoes we finally found a pear of some classy looking combat boots.

"Finally!"

"But you look so beautiful Alice, like a gothic Cinderella."

"Thanks Anne."

Right in the middle of our touching girlfriend moment the doorbell rang.

Anne ran down the stairs to go meet the boy's, yes "boy's". Tonight there was going to be a dance for some reason (or maybe people here are probably celebrating their freedom unconsciously) either way there is a dance tonight and Knight will be taking me, and since Anne and Alex are both left without dates they are going together.

"Alice! Alice! You've got tom come down, your prince is waiting-- and he looks like he about to panic!"

"Ah, your right. Rule number one- don't ever leave your date with your parents alone."

Anne smiled a bog toothy smile, and I suddenly realized something.

"What?"

"Why are you just wearing a ripped T-shirt of *Slayer* and some *Tripp* pants when you should be all dolled up for the dance with Alex?"

"Oh… well Alex said we should just stay at his house and watch some old horror movies."

"Oh…"

I guess it's still a bit awkward between me and him right?

"Did something happen between you two? I mean you guy's haven't talked nor have you guy's made eye contact when you guys do see each other."

"Nothing really. Now if you don't mind, I do need to go help my vampire boyfriend."

I shuffled past Anne, hoping she didn't notice my shamed filled face.

I was finally able to make my way down the stairs, when I saw my Gothic prince just waiting for me by the door.

For a minute Knight looked like he was ready to leave, but when he looked at me all anxiousness left his face.

"You… look really beautiful tonight…"

I looked Knight up and down and I was just breathless. There were no words to describe how handsome he looked.

"You don't look so bad yourself."

'You don't look so bad yourself'? Seriously?! Was that all I could to say about my hot, vampire boyfriend?!

"My you two look so wonderful together."

"Thank you Ma'am."

"Now Mr. Aoi, what time will you be having my daughter back?"

I could feel Knight quiver a bit, so I gently grabbed his hand to calm him down just a bit.

"I shall be having her home before midnight, possibly by ten."

My father nodded in agreement and Knight let out a small sigh of relief.

"Well if you guys don't mind, me and Knight really must be going."

"Wait just one minute Alice! No daughter of mine will be going out in that dress she is in."

"Mother…."

"I mean what if some creepo stalked you home because of the amount of skin your showing… I don't what I would…"

"Mother calm down."

"Don't worry Ma'am, if anyone dares to come near my dear Alice, I can guarantee that there will be blood."

Knight…

"Thank you Knight. Now I feel at ease, but you still have to cover your--"

"Bye mother!"

I quickly grab Knight's hand and lead him out of the house and into the front yard.

Now that I think about it… our front yard looks really flowery… like something out of "*Alice in Wonderland*". Coincidence? I think not!

"Your parent's love you so much."

"Yeah. They just want to catch up you know? For the lost time."

"So what are they like?"

"My parent's? Well let's see… my father is a stern yet quiet type. He's like a sleeping bear. He'll be really sweet and supporting but when it's time to get rough he will become a beast."

I giggle just at the thought of my father becoming a beast.

"And your mother?"

"She's a bit… dramatic. She's like an adult version of Anne."

The walk down the drive way seemed like an eternity. It was like there was something Knight was hiding and I guess it was hard for him to get it out.

It must be something really deep to be troubling-- oh bat's. Don't tell me-- HE'S THINKING OF BREAKING UP WITH ME?!

"Alice?"

After all we've been through?!

"Alice? Are you okay?"

"Of course I'm okay. Why wouldn't I be?!"

Aww crap… I made the situation worse.

"Are you sure your okay?"

"No, no, I'm totally fine. Shall we head to the dance?"

Knight then extended his hand to me and I took it, and as he led me to his black car I could feel myself getting excited yet getting scared.

Knight opened the car door for me and I slowly stepped in, and once he shut the door and went to his side I could feel my chest become tighter.

Will he break up with me at the dance or will he do it after the dance? Ungh, I feel so pathetic...

"So is it just me and you tonight?"

"Yeah. Anne and Alex decided to stay home and watch some horror movies."

"I see."

Knight let out a long sigh. I don't know if it was a sigh of relief or some kind of disappointed sigh.

"Well then how about we ditch the dance then?"

"Why?"

Oh no...

"Because the entire town will be there, and I just want us to be alone."

"I see..."

"Do you not want to be alone?"

As Knight slowed down at a red light I could feel my stomach try to eat itself.

"Alice?"

I finally heard Knight's voice come through and when I looked his face was full of worry and hurt.

"I'm sorry... I didn't hear you..."

It's so hard to look Knight in they eye and not get lost in them.

"I asked if you didn't want to be alone."

"Oh, of course I do! Why wouldn't I be?"

"That's good."

Another sigh…

Maybe I should just enjoy the night while I can.

Knight slowly droved almost across town to an abandoned park. A park that everyone had forgotten about.

The park was already so overgrown with weeds and wild flowers that it almost looked like a small little forest.

"Over here Alice."

I slowly began to follow Knight as he made a path to a large patch of green grass that looks well taken care of.

"Do you like it?"

"Like it? I love it!"

The large patch of green grass may have seemed boring to anyone else, but to me and Knight, who were denizens of the night, we loved it. I especially loved how the moon lit up the large patch, and the glowing bugs made it all the more beautiful.

"Over here."

Knight extended his hand to me and I quickly took it.

Knight gently sat me down in a soft patch of grass and said to wait while he fetched something.

When Knight left I couldn't help but feel beyond happy. He set this whole thing up just for us. If I knew how to sprout wings I would.

"Sorry it took me so long."

"Oh, no prob!"

Knight gently sat down and took out a picnic basket.

"Knight... you didn't have too..."

"Well I wanted to. After all... you are my Alice in my wonderland."

"And you're my Knight in shining armor..."

Knight slowly leaned and then pressed his lips against mine. Suddenly... it didn't mater to me whether he wanted to break up with me or not. I loved Knight with all my heart and I'm not going to let anything happen to us.

"Shall we start the picnic?"

I couldn't say anything so settled with nodding yes.

Before I knew it Knight took out a black lacy blanket and was then taking out some strawberries, some cake and some steaks... raw.

Knight then took out candles and lit them.

"The most romantic dinner with the most gorgeous black rose."

The rest of the night me and Knight ate and talked then we danced to whatever song was in our heads.

When we were too tired we'd rest, but I guess our night together was over. Knight began to pack away everything and I couldn't help but feel down.

"What time is it?"

"It's almost ten."

"Then why are you packing? Can't we just stay like this for a bit longer?"

I know that we can't stay like this... but I just have this feeling. I--

"Alice, is something wrong?"

I suddenly remembered that Knight was still in front of me, and when I looked up he was already by my side, looking worried.

"Nothing I just want to be stay like this."

I quickly gave Knight a hug, hoping he wouldn't notice my worried expression.

Knight suddenly broke our embrace and turned back to packing the picnic.

I think he's actually thinking of breaking up with me...

"Come on Alice, it's time to go."

When Knight said it was time to go I felt lonelier than ever, and my feet felt like they were rooted to the grown.

I don't want this evening to end.

The drive back home was tense, neither Knight nor I wanted to talk.

I guess my fears are real... he's really going to break up with me...

Right before I could wallow in my self misery any longer Knight then pulled up in the drive-way.

This is it then...

"Alice... there's something   I   need   to   sat   to you..."

"I already know."

Knight looked at me quickly then accusingly, and I know that look anywhere. It meant 'Jenny, you told.'.

"No... Jenny didn't tell me, I kind of figured it out."

"How could you have?"

"Come on Knight... it's obvious isn't it? So just spit it out."

"Alice... I didn't know this was going to happen. I'm sorry."

"What do you mean you didn't know this was going to happen? The decision is all up to you."

"The decision is all up to me? If it were up to me then I'd gladly reject the order!"

"Then reject it!"

"I can't!"

Knight's voice was loud and booming, but I stood my ground. It wasn't fair, we should be inseparable after all we've been through, but no! He want's break up because it was an order?! Who on earth would give him such an order?!

"I guess since you know then I guess there's nothing else to say then."

So it's over?!

"Fine. I'm leaving!"

I quickly got out of the car and slammed the door shut. The minute I stormed into the house I ignored my parents questions and stomped upstairs.

Once the door was closed I slowly slid to the ground. Nothing seems real anymore.

I thought Knight loved me… so why?

"Why Knight?"

Before I knew it tears began to form and I began to sob.

Being fast asleep in my dark room all day helped my puffy eyes from crying all night, but it didn't help the situation.

All day I dreamt of Knight and me… and our memories together.

When the dream ended my eyes snapped open… something inside me made my eyes automatically open them. My instincts came in… meaning it was night time.

I finally sat up in my bed and looked around. It only took a few seconds to adjust my eye sight.

Once my eyes were adjusted I threw the covers and went into the bathroom. Right now I wish I could look in the mirror to see how bad I looked from a night of crying.

"Alice? Are you up?"

"Anne?"

I quickly ran out of the bathroom and down the stairs.

Anne was on the couch watching some documentary on *Jack the Ripper*.

"I think they might of finally figured out-- Alice! You look terrible!"

"Gee thanks, that's something I want to hear."

"I'm sorry. Well you don't look terrible, I mean you still look gorgeous even though you just rolled out of bed, but you look like you've been crying."

Anne's face gave it right away that she figured something happened last night.

"Is everything all right?"

Anne gave me a hug and right when she did I folded and cried.

After ten minutes of crying I was finally able to pronounce words.

"So what happened?"

"Last night was great, but I could tell Knight was hiding something. After a great night he said it was time to go, and so when he pulled up in the drive-way he said something to tell."

"So... what he say?"

"To be honest I didn't really let him say it."

"Do you know what he was going to say exactly?"

Come to think of it... I *thought* he was going to break up with me, he never actually said it.

"No... then maybe we still have a chance!"

"Now there's my brave girl! Now let's go fix your puffy eyes and get you dressed."

"For what?"

"For what she says. We're going to get you dressed so you can go over to Knight's and fix everything. Maybe he was trying to say something else."

"Yeah... your right."

Still... that nagging feeling of something being wrong still lurked in my stomach.

"I heard the best way to cure puffy eyes was a hot cloth on it, you know?"

"Sounds good, let's try that."

Anne's matured a bit. I can't help but feel proud, she isn't the little girl who needed help with the simplest things anymore.

After thirty minutes, I decided that just a black shirt and jeans would be good enough.

"Alright Alice, go get your undead man back!"

"Thanks Anne…"

After a few encouraging words from Anne, I ran out the door faster than light.

It's night, I don't think anyone will notice my vampire speed, right?

Finally talking myself into doing vampire speed I sped up my pace. It seemed like hours had passed by when I finally got to Knight's large, looming mansion.

"Okay… no need to be all nervous. It's not like he actually broke up with me."

I never knew five minutes of inhaling and exhaling would actually help a person calm down.

Now, if only I could rack up the nerve to ring the doorbell.

Oh for crying out loud! It's just a--

The door suddenly swung open and out popped out my favorite maid.

"Good evening Alice."

"Hey Jen, umm is Knight here?"

"Huh? No…"

"Oh…"

I guess he doesn't want to see me after all.

"Did Master Knight not tell you?"

"Tell me what? That he actually wanted to break up with me?"

"No! Ungh, come in Alice we need to talk."

I slowly walked, feeling more confused than sad.

"Wait, what are you talking about Jenny?"

"Last night, when you guys went to the dance he was supposed to tell you about him departing."

"Departing?"

"Yes. His mission here is done and the original idea was to just return back to the vampire society, but for obvious reasons he has gone to tell them that he will remain here."

My face felt so hot, so hot in fact that I thought I was in hell.

"So that's why he was a bit down…"

Right when I hear the those words tears form and suddenly fell.

I was happy that Knight still loved me, but sad that he had to leave… and ashamed for thinking something so stupid…

"Oh dear, um, let me get you some tissues!"

Knight still truly loves me, and he wanted to stay here, and that's what he was trying to say last night. It wasn't his choice, it was the Vampire Elder's choice.

Knight was supposed to go back, but because of me he wants to stay.

How could I say such things to Knight? I'm the worst…

"Alice, here. I brought some tissues."

I looked up at Jenny and began to cry again. I can't imagine a world without Jenny. Jenny never left my side, and she never judged me no matter how many people or vampires judged her, and I can't especially think of a world with no Knight.

My heart would just break…

"Alice…"

No matter how hard I tried to stop crying the tears kept coming.

I'm so ashamed… Knight… I'm sorry…

"He will be back by summers end, so you'll see Master Knight then."

I then dried my tears and blew my nose. Knight will be coming back so when he does I will apologize to him and give him a heartfelt kiss.